Also by Gerald Murnane

FICTION

Tamarisk Row
A Lifetime on Clouds
The Plains
Landscape with Landscape
Inland
Velvet Waters
Emerald Blue
Barley Patch
A History of Books
A Million Windows
Stream System

NONFICTION

Invisible Yet Enduring Lilacs
Something for the Pain

Border Districts

Border Districts

A

Fiction

Gerald Murnane

FARRAR, STRAUS AND GIROUX   NEW YORK

Farrar, Straus and Giroux
175 Varick Street, New York 10014

Copyright © 2017 by Gerald Murnane
All rights reserved
Printed in the United States of America
Originally published in Australia in 2017 by Giramondo Publishing,
New South Wales
Published in the United States by Farrar, Straus and Giroux
First American edition, 2018

Library of Congress Cataloging-in-Publication Data
Names: Murnane, Gerald, 1939– author.
Title: Border districts : a fiction / Gerald Murnane.
Description: First American edition. | New York : Farrar, Straus and Giroux,
2018.
Identifiers: LCCN 2017038330 | ISBN 9780374115753 (hardcover) |
ISBN 9780374717278 (ebook)
Subjects: LCSH: Reminiscing—Fiction. | Memory—Fiction. | Reflection
Classification: LCC PR9619.3.M76 B67 2018 | DDC 823/.914—dc23
LC record available at https://lccn.loc.gov/2017038330

Designed by Abby Kagan

Our books may be purchased in bulk for promotional, educational, or business
use. Please contact your local bookseller or the Macmillan Corporate
and Premium Sales Department at 1-800-221-7945, extension 5442,
or by e-mail at MacmillanSpecialMarkets@macmillan.com.

www.fsgbooks.com
www.twitter.com/fsgbooks • www.facebook.com/fsgbooks

1   3   5   7   9   10   8   6   4   2

Border Districts

Two months ago, when I first arrived in this township just short of the border, I resolved to guard my eyes, and I could not think of going on with this piece of writing unless I were to explain how I came by that odd expression.

I got some of my schooling from a certain order of religious brothers, a band of men who dressed each in a black soutane with a bib of white celluloid at his throat. I learned by chance last year, and fifty years since I last saw anyone wearing such a thing, that the white bib was called a *rabat* and was a symbol of chastity. Among the few books that I brought here from the capital city is a large dictionary, but the word *rabat* is not listed in it. The word may well be French, given that the order of brothers was founded in France. In this remote district, I am even less inclined than I was in the suburbs of the capital city to seek out some or another obscure fact; here, near the border, I am even more inclined than of old to accept as well-founded any supposition likely to complete a pattern in my mind and then to go on writing until I learn the meaning for me of such an image as that of the white patch which appeared just now against a black ground at the edge of my mind and will not be easily dislodged.

The school where the brothers taught was built in the grounds of what had been a two-storey mansion of yellow sandstone in a street lined with plane-trees in an inner eastern suburb of the capital city. The mansion itself had been converted into the brothers' residence. On the ground floor of the former mansion, one of the rooms overlooking the return veranda was the chapel, which was used by the brothers for their daily mass and prayers but was available also to us, their students.

In the language of that place and time, a student who called at the chapel for a few minutes was said to be paying a visit. The object of his visitation was said to be Jesus in the Blessed Sacrament or, more commonly, the Blessed Sacrament. We boys were urged by teachers and priests to pay frequent visits to the Blessed Sacrament. It was implied that the personage denoted by that phrase would feel aggrieved or lonely if visitors were lacking. My class once heard from a religious brother one of a sort of story that was often told in order to promote our religious zeal. A non-Catholic of good will had asked a priest to explain the teachings of the Church in the matter of the Blessed Sacrament. The priest then explained how every disc of consecrated bread in every tabernacle in every Catholic church or chapel, even though it appeared to be mere bread, was in substance the body of Jesus Christ, the Second Person of the Blessed Trinity. The inquirer of good will then declared that if only he were able to believe this, he would spend every free moment in some or another Catholic church or chapel, in the presence of the divine manifestation.

In our school magazine every year, in his annual report to parents, our principal wrote at length about what he called the religious formation of us boys. In every classroom, the first period of every day was given over to Christian Doctrine, or religion, as we more often called it. Students recited aloud together a short prayer before every period of the daily timetable. I believed that most of my classmates took their religion seriously, but I seldom heard any boy make any mention, outside the classroom, of anything to do with that religion. The chapel was out of sight of the playground, and so I was never aware of how many of my classmates paid visits there. However, I went through several periods of religious fervour during my schooldays, and during each such period I paid several visits daily to the Blessed Sacrament. Sometimes I saw one or another of my classmates in the chapel, kneeling as I knelt with head bowed or eyes fixed on the locked tabernacle, within which, and out of our sight, was the gold-plated ciborium filled with the white wafers that we thought of as the Blessed Sacrament. I was never satisfied with my attempts to pray or to contemplate, and I often wondered what exactly was taking place in the mind of my devout-seeming classmate. I would have liked to ask him what he seemed to see while he prayed; how he envisaged the divine or canonised personages that he addressed in his mind, and much else. Sometimes, by chance, a classmate and I would leave the chapel at the same time and would walk together along the return veranda and then through the brothers' garden towards the playground, but for me to have questioned the boy then about his devotions would have been hardly less disturbing than if I had made him an indecent proposition.

In the quiet street where I now live is a tiny church that I pass every weekday morning on my walk to the shops and the post office. The church belongs to one of the Protestant denominations that I pitied as a schoolboy on account of the drabness of their services, which consisted, I supposed, of mere hymns and sermons and none of the splendid rituals enacted in my own church. Whenever I pass, the grass around my neighbourhood church is always neatly mown but the church itself is closed and deserted. I must have passed countless Protestant churches in suburbs or in country towns and scarcely glanced at them, and yet I can never pass the nearby church without my thoughts being led in surprising directions.

I have always believed myself to be indifferent to architecture. I hardly know what a gable is or a nave or a vault or a vestry. I would describe my neighbourhood church as a symmetrical building comprising three parts: a porch, a main part, and, at the furthest end from the street, a third part surely reserved for the minister before and after services. The walls are of stone painted—or is the correct term *rendered*?—a uniform creamy white. I am so unobservant of such details that I cannot recall, here at my desk, whether the pitched roofs of the porch and the main part are of slate or of iron. The rear part has an almost flat iron roof. The windows aren't of much interest to me, except for the two rectangular windows of clear glass, each with a drawn blind behind it, in the rear wall

6

of the minister's room. The main part of the church has six small windows, three on each side. The glass in each of these windows is translucent. If I could inspect it from close at hand, the glass might well seem no different from the sort that I learned to call as a child *frosted* and saw often in bathroom windows. The glass in the six windows is by no means colourless, but I have not yet identified the shade or tint that distinguishes it.

On some mornings when I pass, the glass in question seems an unexceptional grey-green or, perhaps, grey-blue. Once, however, when I happened to pass the church in the late afternoon, and when I looked over my shoulder at a window on the shaded, south-eastern side of the building, I saw the glass there coloured not directly by the setting sun but by a light that I was prevented from seeing: the glow within the locked church where the rays from the west had already been modified by the three windows on the side further from me. Even if I could have devised a name for the wavering richness that I saw then in that simple pane, I would have had to set about devising soon afterwards a different name for the subtly different tint in each of its two neighbouring panes, where the already muted light from one and the same sunset had been separately refracted. The porch has one window, which looks towards the street. This is the window that mostly takes my notice as I pass and may well have been the cause of my setting out to write these pages. The glass in this window is what I have always called stained glass and almost certainly comprises a representation of something—a pattern of leaves and stems and petals perhaps. I prefer not to draw attention to myself when I walk in the township, and I have not yet been bold enough to stop and stare at the porch window. I am unsure not only of what is depicted there but even of the colours of the different zones of glass, although I suppose they are red and green and yellow and blue or most of those. The outer door of the church is always closed when I pass, and the door from the porch to the church is surely also closed. Since the tinted window faces north-east, the near side of the glass is always in bright daylight while the far side is opposed only to the subdued light of the enclosed porch. Anyone looking from my well-lit vantage-point can only guess at the colours of the glass and the details of what they depict.

Perhaps thirty years ago, I read a review of a scholarly book in which part of the text comprised extracts from diaries kept by several men who travelled throughout England during the years of the Commonwealth smashing stained-glass windows. The men stood on ladders and used staves or axes to smash the glass. They reported in their diaries the name of each church that they visited and the numbers of windows that they smashed. They declared often in the diaries that they were doing the work of the Lord or promoting his glory. I have never travelled more than a day's journey by road or rail from my birthplace. Foreign countries exist for me as mental images, some of them vivid and detailed and many of them having originated while I was reading works of fiction. My image of England is of a mostly green topographical map, richly detailed but comparatively small for an image-country. While I was reading the review of the book mentioned, I wondered how any stained-glass windows could have been left in the country after the men mentioned had done their widespread work. I wondered too what had become of all the smashed glass. I supposed the men had attacked the windows from the outside—had rammed their staves and axes against the dull-seeming glass without knowing what it represented or even what were its colours as seen from the other side.

For how long were the coloured chunks and shards left to lie in the aisles and on the pews? Were the smashed pieces gathered up by the dismayed congregation and hidden against a time when they could be melted or otherwise turned again into images of revered personages in other-worldly settings? Did children carry off handfuls of many-coloured chips and afterwards squint through them at trees or sky or try to arrange them as they had formerly been or to guess whether this or that fragment had once represented part of a trailing robe, a radiant halo, an enraptured countenance?

According to the history taught to me as a child, the images in the smashed windows were expressions of the old faith of England. The glass designs had outlasted by a century the prayers and ceremonies and vestments that had been done away with during the Protestant Revolt, as we were taught to call it. If I had read during my schooldays about the smashing of the glass, I might well have regretted the destruction of so many admirable images but I would have considered that the glassless windows were no less than the traitorous Protestants deserved. The empty window-spaces would have suggested to me the sightless eyes of a people blind to the truth. They had abolished coloured chasubles, gold monstrances, the Blessed Sacrament itself. Now let them sing and sermonise in black soutanes and white surplices and in the plain light of day, unstained by any glass of olden times. I would hardly have thought thus as I read during my adulthood about the smashers of windows, but my first sight of the window in the porch of my neighbourhood church caused me to feel a slight resentment that a Protestant sect founded not even three centuries ago should ornament their simple place of worship in the style of the church that had lasted for nearly two millennia before the beginnings of their upstart faction. Even the surroundings of the small stone building made me somewhat resentful. No footpath leads past the church. Between the roadside kerb and the boundary of the churchyard, the ground is uneven beneath the mown grass. Not wanting to stop and stare as I pass, I have to learn what I can while fearing to turn an ankle.

What I learned a month ago from my first sight of the church I reported in an earlier paragraph. Until this morning, I had learned no more. I did not even know whether services were still held in the church. (The Anglican and the Lutheran churches, small weatherboard buildings, have each a notice outside showing the date and time of the next service. The weatherboard Catholic church was demolished a few months before I arrived here; the building had been infested with termites and was deemed unsafe.) This morning, I got ready for my first trip across the border. I was going to set out for a race-meeting in a town named for its closeness to the border. While the engine in my car was running, I went to open the front gate. A row of cars was parked in front of the church. Apparently, a service was being held. I can hardly explain even now why I did so, but I switched off the engine in my car and set out walking slowly towards the church as though I was taking a morning stroll. I counted the churchgoers' cars easily enough.

There were seven. They were all large, late-model cars such as are owned by the farmers in the districts around this township. I surmised that each car had brought a middle-aged couple to church. Perhaps a few persons had walked to the church from houses in the township, but the congregation could hardly have numbered twenty. I heard no sound when I first strolled past the church, but on my way back I heard singing and the sound of a musical instrument. I had always supposed that the denomination whose church it was sang joyously, wholeheartedly. Admittedly, I was ten paces from the back porch, but the rear door of the church and the outer door of the porch had been left open on account of the heat, and yet the singing still sounded faintly and almost timidly. The voices of the congregation hardly rose above the sound of the imitation organ, or whatever they called the instrument accompanying them. I wrote *the voices of the congregation* just then, but they sounded to me to be all female voices. If the men were singing, they could not be heard outside the walls of the building.

I moved to this district near the border so that I could spend most of my time alone and so that I could live according to several rules that I had for long wanted to live by. I mentioned earlier that I guard my eyes. I do this so that I might be more alert to what appears at the edges of my range of vision; so that I might notice at once any sight so much in need of my inspection that one or more of its details seems to quiver or to be agitated until I have the illusion that I am being signalled to or winked at. Another rule requires me to record whatever sequences of images occur to me after I have turned my attention to the signalling or winking detail. I was preparing this morning to travel across the border but I put off my departure and went inside to my desk and made notes for what is reported at length in the paragraphs hereabout.

During one of the last years of the 1940s, I was taken by my parents on many a Sunday to a small timber church in the south-western district of this state. At each side of the church were two long timber poles. One end of each pole was fixed in the ground; the other end rested firmly against the upper wall of the church. I assumed that the poles kept the church from leaning or even toppling. The building thus kept upright comprised a tiny porch; a main part with a railed-off sanctuary and perhaps twelve pews divided by a central aisle; and a small room for the use of a priest. The congregation of the church comprised mostly farmers and their families. A custom was followed in that church such as I never observed in any other. In the timber church with the four poles, the pews on the left, or the Gospel side, were occupied only by male persons while the pews on the right, or the Epistle side, were occupied only by females. I never saw anyone violate this strict segregation. Once, two newcomers, a young husband and wife, went in early and sat together on the men's side. The church was not even half full before the wife understood her mistake. She hurried across the aisle, blushing, and joined the other women and the girls.

Many years later, while I was reading a magazine article about the Christian sect known as the Shakers, an image formed in my mind of a group of adult worshippers in a small timber building hardly different from the church mentioned in the previous paragraph. It was mostly an incongruous image, lit by the sunlight of a summer morning in southern Australia. The male worshippers wore dark suits and wide neckties, and their faces and necks and hands and wrists were red-brown. The females wore floral patterned dresses and large hats of lacquered straw. The males and the females stood facing each other, not in pews but in choir stalls. Their standing in stalls prevented them from performing the sedate dance that I had read about in the article on the Shakers. This seemed to consist of two lines of dancers advancing towards one another and then retreating a little; advancing further still but then again retreating. One line, of course, was of men and the other of women. While they danced, they chanted or, perhaps, sang. In the magazine article were two lines of one of their best-known songs—or was it their only song?

> *Shake, shake, shake along, Dan'l!*
> *Shake out of me all things carnal!*

The Shakers would have sung this with sincerity; they aspired to celibacy. The men and the women of each community were required to live apart.

Many of the men and women in my fanciful image were husbands and wives, but these too sang softly the two lines of the old Shaker song. Rather, the women sang while the men merely mouthed the words. It was well known that male Catholic churchgoers could hardly ever be induced to sing. Nor did the men in my image seem to move their bodies, although the

13

women swayed in time to their chanting and some even made as though to lean or to step towards the chest-high wooden wall that barred their way.

The same small church was also the setting, many years ago, for the mental events that originated while I was reading one of a collection of short stories from a book that I long ago disposed of. I have forgotten the title of the book and I remember nothing of what was in my mind while I read the book except for a few mental scenes, so to call them. I bought and read the book because the author had been at one time a colleague of mine in an obscure department on an out-of-the-way campus of a lesser university. He was one of a not insignificant body of men to be met with in the last decades of the twentieth century: men who were pleased to have it known that they had formerly been Catholic priests or religious brothers. Some were teachers or librarians or public servants; a few worked as journalists or as radio or television producers; and a few were even published authors. Most of the books by these last-mentioned had a preachy tone; their authors were still driven to rectify, or at least to deplore, seeming wrongs in society, which last was one of their most frequently used words.

In the unimaginable circumstance that I were writing a work of fiction with a representation of my one-time colleague as one of its characters, I would feel obliged to report to my putative readers his motives for having abandoned a calling that he had formally vowed to follow for life. Whatever crises of conscience I might attribute to the character, and however detailed and wordy might be my accounts of his purported thinking and feeling, I would report at some point in my narrative that the man did what he did for the reason that he had found he was able to do it.

I have long subscribed to a simple explanation for the defection of so many priests and religious from what might be called my own generation. I can allow that the first daring few might have been pioneers of a sort, devisers of original moral issues, but those who came after them were mere followers of fashion. Once having learned from the example of their more daring fellows that so-called solemn vows could be set aside or broken at no great cost, they who had once sworn to be chaste and obedient set about indulging their restlessness or curiosity.

I seem to remember that several of my former colleague's short stories had a priest as chief character. The only story that has stayed in my mind seemed to have no other meaning than to point up the unseemly awe that many lay persons felt towards priests in the 1960s, when the story was set. The priest in the story may have been the first-person narrator—I forget. He was certainly the chief character and almost the only character apart from a middle-aged woman of a kind once common in Catholic parishes. Holy-water hens they were sometimes called. As I recall it, the priest was visiting the small country church for the first time to celebrate Sunday mass. When he arrived, his bladder happened to be uncomfortably full. Every country church has a men's and a women's toilet in separate rear corners of the churchyard. Why did the priest in the story not visit the men's toilet as soon as he had arrived? I do not know, but if he had done so, my former colleague would have had no story to write. What happened, so to speak, was that the priest was met at the church door by the holy-water hen, who then accompanied him into the sacristy so that she could show him where things were stored. Instead of then leaving discreetly, the woman began prattling to the priest about parish matters or, perhaps, her own concerns. Again, questions arise: Why did the priest not ask the woman politely to leave? Why did he not simply excuse himself and visit the toilet? The story probably depended on the young priest's being too nervous to dismiss the older woman or to cause her to recall that although he was one of God's anointed, he had still a body that functioned as did other men's bodies. The woman went on talking; the priest went on listening politely while his bladder ached. At last, he was able by some or another means to get rid of the woman. Perhaps she left of her own accord. Even then, however, the priest's misery was not over. He flung open one after another cupboard in search of something that he could urinate into. The last sentence of the story reported his immense relief as he filled with his urine a bottle containing a small quantity of so-called altar wine for use in the ceremony of the mass.

Recalling the silly story today for the first time in nearly thirty years I see not some fictional priest but my colleague of long ago dressed as I had never seen him in a black suit with a white celluloid collar at his throat and holding above his head a bottle labelled *Seven Hills Altar Wine*. He holds the bottle between himself and a single east-facing window while he stares in through the brightly lit red-brown glass. Through the wall he hears the shuffling and the throat-clearing of the farmers and their wives and children as they file into the church and settle themselves—men and boys on the Gospel side; women and girls on the Epistle side. Through another wall, he hears the heaving in the wind of the gum trees that border the grassy churchyard or the clinking calls of rosellas.

Why have I recalled today a piece of writing that I surely dismissed when I first read it: an embellished retelling of something that perhaps befell the author during his years as a priest? Why have I included in this report the tedious matter of the preceding paragraphs? One answer may be that I have learned to trust the promptings of my mind, which urges me sometimes to study in all seriousness matters that another person might dismiss as unworthy, trivial, childish. The discomfort of the fictional priest and the predictable motives of the pestering woman have long since settled among my own concerns, one of which might be called the life and death of mental entities. The author of the short story would have stood alone in many a sacristy in many a tiny church with parrots in the trees around and would have bowed his head and prayed that the ceremony he was about to perform and the sermon he was about to preach would bring nearer to God the persons coughing and shuffling just then on the far side of the sanctuary rails. Robed in his white or scarlet or green or violet chasuble, the young man would have sensed the presence of a personage that he took to be the creator of the universe and at the same time the friend and confidant of anyone who approached him from among the countless millions of the living but especially those who had been ordained as priests of the church founded by His only son. It should be clear from some of the earliest paragraphs of this report that I would very much like to know what the young priest saw in his mind at such a time. I intend to mention later an autobiography published after the death of the short-story writer and former priest. Much of the writing in the posthumous book is frank and candid, but nowhere in it does the author try to describe what interests me most about his sort of person; nowhere does he report his religious experiences.

I strayed a little in the previous two sentences. I intended to remark on the great difference between the concerns of the young priest and those of the author of the short story, the one constantly aware of the presence of God and the other only wanting to make clumsy humour at the expense of his younger self. I intended to ask what had become of the imagined presence or personage who had ruled the life of the young man. I am not judging the writer but rather marvelling that a powerful image-in-the-mind could thus seem to have lapsed into irrelevance.

Even while my sometime colleague, the former priest, was writing his fiction, the persons who had once respected him or been in awe of him would have been reading in newspapers the first of many accounts that they would read of priests found guilty at law of deeds incomparably graver than urinating into altar-wine bottles in sacristies. How many of those who read such reports decided at once, or after much reflection, that they no longer considered sacred some of the persons, places, and things that they had previously deemed so. I heard once from one such person, a woman who had gone to church every Sunday until she underwent the experiences reported below.

The woman worked as the receptionist and secretary of a

psychiatrist. One day, her employer had asked her to type into his computer the contents of several long statements by a young woman who was making some or another claim for reparation from her local diocese. The woman my informant was middle-aged, married, and a mother, but her employer told her that she need not finish typing the statements if she found the contents distressing. The woman told me that she found the contents most distressing, although she typed all of them. She told me about the statements only that they were reports of acts of sexual abuse perpetrated against the author of the statements by a priest during several years of her childhood. The woman told me this in a crowded lounge-bar of a hotel late during an evening when she and her husband and my wife and I and several other couples were drinking after a day at a race-meeting. I cannot be sure that I did not hear from the woman that the girl's sister had also been sexually abused or that more than one priest was involved. Although the woman thought often about the contents of the statements during the months after she had typed them, her routine continued as before and she attended church every Sunday. She attended church also for the funeral of an elderly woman, a friend of her family. The funeral service was a so-called concelebrated mass, with three priests together at the altar. Such a ceremony is an honour reserved for priests themselves, close relatives of priests, or lay persons who have given long service to one or another parish or religious order, as my informant's elderly friend had done. Several times during such a ceremony, the priests bow in unison towards the altar or towards each other. At one point in the ceremony, they take turns to swing towards the altar and then towards each other a brass thurible out of which rises the smoke from burning incense. The woman told me quietly in the noisy lounge-bar that she felt increasingly distressed as the concelebrated service went forward, and that a moment had arrived when she was driven to get up from her seat and to leave the church. At that moment, the chief celebrant had bowed low over the altar. His co-celebrants, standing on either side of him and with hands pressed together beneath their chins, had each made his own slight bow and had then looked on gravely while the celebrant kissed the white altar-cloth. The concelebrated mass had taken place several months ago, the woman told me. She had not stepped inside a church since then and she intended never again to do so.

How many times since I first heard the woman's story have I tried to appreciate the notable mental events that must have followed her walking away from the ceremonious gesturing of the priests? If only I had had the wit to ask the woman on that evening in the lounge-bar what she supposed had become of the imagery connected with her lifelong beliefs, would I then have glimpsed for myself a version of her seeming to see the colour draining from the tall glass windows in the church where she had prayed since childhood? the layers of vestments being stripped from the men who had vowed to be chaste? the withdrawal of the favourite image of her loving saviour into the mental regions where flitted or wavered the figures of myth or legend?

Whenever I tried long ago to learn from books about the workings of minds, I was equally troubled whether I read fiction or non-fiction. In the same way that I struggled and failed to follow plots and to comprehend the motives of characters, so did I struggle to follow arguments and to understand concepts. I failed as a reader of fiction because I was constantly engaged not with the seeming subject-matter of the text but with the doings of personages who appeared to me while I tried to read and with the scenery that appeared around them. My image-world was often only slightly connected with the text in front of my eyes; anyone privy to my seeming sights might have supposed I was reading some barely recognisable variant of the text, a sort of apocrypha of the published work. As a reader of texts intended to explain the mind, I failed because the words and phrases in front of my eyes gave rise only to the poorest sort of image. Reading about *our minds* or *the mind*, and about purported instincts or aptitudes or faculties, not to mention such phantasms as *ego*, *id*, and *archetype*, I supposed the endless-seeming landscapes of my own thoughts and feelings must have been a paradise by comparison with the drab sites where others located their selves or their personalities or whatever they called their mental territories. And so, I decided long ago to take no further interest in the theoretical and to study instead the actual, which was for me the seeming scenery behind everything I did or thought or read.

The previous sentence might seem to suggest that I began early in life to observe coolly whatever I took to be the contents of my mind. No, for much of my life I barely found time to observe, let alone reflect on, the teeming mental imagery that accumulated by the minute, even though I often supposed that some or another distinctive image-item might one day be the only evidence that I had not only lived at some or another time in some or another place but had known and felt as though I was doing so. Now, at last, in this quiet township near the border, I am free to record my own image-history, which includes, of course, my speculations about such image-events as unfolded while a little-known author of fiction seemed to recall from all the years when he had prayed and worshipped daily only a morning when he had urinated into some altar-wine, or such as had unfolded when a certain woman, a life-long believer, saw, during a funeral service, not the admirable details of a solemn ritual but something that had caused her to turn away in disgust.

I may not have gone far with the speculations mentioned just now, but I am able to report much about certain of my own experiences that came to mind while I was writing the previous paragraphs. At the age of twenty, while I was reading one or another of the novels of Thomas Hardy, I was startled to find that I had done quietly and calmly what I had often been warned I was likely to do if I read the works of atheists or agnostics or pantheists or almost any sort of writer of fiction apart from G. K. Chesterton, Hilaire Belloc, and Ethel Mannin and, perhaps, François Mauriac. Exactly what my teachers and pastors and parents had predicted had happened: I had read indiscriminately and, as a result, I had lost my religious faith. Why I should have suffered this loss while reading Thomas Hardy is no part of this report, although I cannot resist including here something that I read only a few years ago in some or another essay or article. According to G. K. Chesterton, so I read, to read the fiction of Thomas Hardy is to witness the village atheist's brooding and blaspheming over the village idiot.

The loss of my faith, to call it that, brought about many changes in my way of life, only one of which is relevant here. From the day when the loss took place (and it did indeed happen within a single day) I possessed a host of mental images that were no longer of use to me. I had previously considered these images the nearest available likenesses of personages by definition invisible to me. I could never have prayed if I had not been able to bring the images to mind. Now, they were of no account: mere images corresponding to nothing in any world of other-than-images. And yet they survived, undiminished. Those that had always appeared to me as depictions in stained glass were still lit by the same glow from their further sides. Those that had seemed to well up from what I had formally called my immortal soul still floated, as it were, near the image of that now-non-existent item and were still able to confront me whenever I was baffled or afraid, as though I was about to pray as I had so often prayed in the past to the beings they denoted. Chief among these now-useless possessions was my image of the so-called Blessed Trinity, the creator and sustainer of the universe, who was one indivisible divinity but nevertheless comprised three persons. (No phrase or sentence hereabouts is intended to mock.) I had never succeeded in fixing in mind an image of this tripartite being: I had mostly to be satisfied with seeing each person as the occupant of his own seat on a throne designed for three. In the central seat was a white-bearded ancient. I struggled not to visualize him thus. I told myself often that God was a spirit and was therefore impossible to represent pictorially, but I had been too much influenced as a child by the line-drawings in my missal or by reproductions of celebrated paintings of grandfatherly cloud-dwellers. (While I was writing the previous sentences, I was sorry to be reporting such a commonplace experience. I was ashamed to have been as a boy and as a youth so easily influenced by the details of trite illustrations. I believed I could have described a more interesting sort of mental imagery if only those sentences had been part of a work of fiction. I even tried to devise a means of including in this report the details of the image in my mind of an image reported in a book that I first read nearly forty years ago. The first-person narrator of that book, which is not a work of fiction, had seen as a boy, in the kitchen of a Hungarian peasant household during the first decade of the twentieth century, a framed illustration in which the First Person of the Trinity was depicted as a large eye enclosed within a triangle. I would have been pleased to have been the author of a work of fiction in which the chief character kept in mind, as a boy and as a youth, just such an image of the personage known to him as God the Father. As the author of such a work, I would have taken much time in deciding what might have been the colour of the iris of the image-eye: a rich orange-gold, perhaps, or an aloof, cool green. I might have included in the work at least one account of the chief character's seeing in the eye the same rich colour that he had lately stared at in some or another sunlit pane of glass in some or another silent building.) My image of the Son was derived from some or another illustration of the Good Shepherd or the Light of the World, but even though he was much younger,

24

the brown-bearded and pensive-eyed son-in-my-mind seemed hardly less forbidding than the father. According to the doctrine of the incarnation, the personage that I knew as Jesus or Christ was at the same time both man and god, and my speculating on this made me often resentful. He whose words and deeds were reported in the Gospels seemed on too familiar a footing with his god to be truly human. Jesus the man ought to have been repelled by the images of stern old men that occurred to him whenever he tried to pray; he ought to have struggled continually to visualise more appropriate images of his god. (Seemingly, I overlooked as a boy the many complexities of the incarnation. I cannot recall wondering how Jesus visualised his own divine nature: what image he called to mind of the god that he himself was.)

The Holy Ghost, called nowadays the Holy Spirit, was sometimes referred to as the forgotten person of the Blessed Trinity. Not only did I never forget him; he was by far my favourite of the three divine persons. When I was in my tenth year and attending a school conducted by a different order of brothers from those mentioned earlier, my class teacher was a young layman who was in love with the Virgin Mary. He claimed no more than to have a special devotion to the Blessed Virgin, as he mostly called her, but I, who was continually falling in love with personages known to me only from illustrations in newspapers or magazines or from fictional texts— I never doubted that my teacher was truly in love. More than thirty years later, while I was reading some or another passage in the fiction of Marcel Proust about the odd ways of some or another character in love, I remembered that my teacher of long ago would use any pretext for bringing the name of his beloved into classroom discussions. I sensed that my class-mates were embarrassed by our teacher's special devotion, as he called it, but I felt a certain sympathy for him. I was not in love with Mary, but I felt as though I ought to have been so. Of course, the name *Mary* hereabouts denotes a mental image. My trouble was that I had never seen on any picture or statue of Mary such a face as I was apt to fall in love with. More than ten years later, I saw too late just such a face as would have won me over earlier. I have not forgotten that this paragraph began as an account of my liking for the Holy Ghost.

At about the time when I was reading for the first time one after another of the novels of Thomas Hardy, a younger cousin of mine showed me a book that he had received as a prize for his results in Christian Doctrine at the same secondary school that I had attended a few years earlier. The title of the book, as I recall, was *The Great Madonnas*. The contents included the reproductions of photographs of numerous paintings and statues of Mary from many countries and many periods of history. The image that I fell in love with was of a young woman with dark hair and a pale complexion. Had I seen that image only a few months before, when I was still a faithful churchgoer, I would have been able to think of myself, at last, as having a special devotion to the Blessed Virgin just as the young man, my teacher, had had. But the image of the dark-haired young woman was not lost on me; it became for me the image-in-my-mind of the chief female character of whatever novel by Thomas Hardy I was reading at that time. As for the one or two novels that I had read before I saw the compelling image, whatever earlier images of female characters had occurred to me were gone from my mind as soon as I had seen the dark-haired madonna, who was thenceforth my image-heroine.

The title of the painting the reproduction of which had so affected me was *Mater Purissima*. This, as I knew, was a Latin phrase equivalent in English to *Mother Most Pure*. The painter was an Englishman of the late nineteenth or the early twentieth century whose name I forgot almost as soon as I had read it. Although the reproduction was in black and white, I was sometimes able to visualise a coloured version of the image of the young woman. It occurs to me today that the original of the painted image may well have been posed so that her face and shoulders were lit by a broad shaft of sunlight that had reached her by way of some or another translucent window high above her and out of the scope of the painting. In my coloured version this light would surely have been a rich red-gold. The young woman was depicted as being clothed in an ankle-length robe with a transparent veil over her hair and holding a dove in each hand. Her hands were so positioned that each dove rested against one of her breasts. When I first took note of these doves, I supposed them to be sacrificial offerings that the young Mary was obliged to make in some or another ritual soon after she had given birth to the child Jesus.

However, I was like most members of my church in knowing little or nothing about the Jewish religion, and so I soon found other connotations for the doves. (I seem not to have noticed what I most notice now when I recall the image-birds:

their improbable docility; they rest comfortably in the hands of the young woman with their own rounded breasts suggesting the shape of what lies hidden behind them under the folds of the young woman's robe and with their bright eyes focused, so it seems, on the same point of interest that the Most Pure Mother looks towards. Their pose is absurdly calm; they bear no resemblance to any of the struggling, frantic birds that I sometimes tried to hold as a boy.)

The young teacher with the special devotion to Mary had once read, so he told us, that she was the daughter-in-law of God the Father and the wife of the Holy Ghost. I was startled at the time by the word *wife*. I considered it unseemly to think of Mary even as the wife of Joseph. The teacher's bold statement stayed in my mind, however, and was the cause of my acquiring in later years a cluster of odd images that helped me comprehend the mystery of Mary's having conceived the Son of God. The formula most often used in the liturgy had Mary conceiving *by the power of the Holy Ghost*. I seem to recall illustrations of a young woman with her head bowed while the Holy Ghost hovers above her in the form of a dove, which was the image most commonly used to illustrate the presence of the third person of the Trinity. I have never learned the origin of the connection between the dove and the Holy Ghost, but for many years I never questioned its appropriateness. In the streets and gardens of the suburbs where I spent much of my childhood, one of the most common birds was a species of dove introduced long ago into this country from Asia. During spring or summer, I would often watch a male dove courting a female by fluttering in the air around her while she, seemingly indifferent to him, perched on a wire or a branch. The fluttering might last for ten minutes before the male would try to mount the female while she clung to her narrow perch. Invariably, he failed. He would likewise fail at one after another later attempt. If ever I witnessed a successful mating between two doves, I must later have forgotten it, which seems unlikely. I believe rather that I had never enough time or patience to go on watching the birds. The dove that was the image in my mind of the Holy Ghost was a more splendid bird by far than the suburban doves; his plumage was orange-red like the tongues of flame that had been the visible sign of his presence when he appeared to Jesus's disciples in the upper room at Pentecost. But for all his fine feathers and his divine powers, he went on fluttering, whenever I brought him to mind, far above the bowed head of his virgin-wife.

Although I saw the illustration of the painting *Mater Purissima* only two or three times, I never afterwards doubted that a certain image-face in my mind was derived wholly from my few inspections of the black and white illustration. Nearly forty years after I had last looked into my cousin's book, and while I was reading one or another biography of Thomas Hardy, I found among the illustrations in that book a reproduction of a black and white photograph of a young woman whose face seemed to me identical with the face of the young woman holding the doves. The young woman photographed was an actress who played the part of Tess Durbeyfield in a dramatisation of the novel *Tess of the D'Urbervilles* during the second decade of the twentieth century. The dramatisation was done under the supervision of Thomas Hardy himself, who was at that time even older than I am as I write these words. Hardy was deemed by his wife and by others to have fallen in love, during the eighth decade of his life, with the young actress, who was fifty years his junior. He declared to several persons that the actress was identical in appearance with the image in his mind of the fictional character, Tess Durbeyfield.

While I was writing the previous paragraph, I was prompted to look again at the photograph of the young actress and to compare that image with the image presently in my mind, but then I recalled that I had sold most of my books before moving from the city where I had lived for most of my life to this township near the border. I had sold the books because this house where I now live is a mere cottage with space for only a few hundred books. I had sold the books also in order to keep faith with myself. For some years past, I had claimed that whatever deserved to be remembered from my experiences as a reader of books was, in fact, safely remembered. I had claimed also the converse of this: whatever I had forgotten from my experiences as a reader of books had not deserved to be remembered. By selling my books, I was declaring that I had got from them whatever I had needed from them. I had therefore no business to be looking back through any biography of any writer of fiction in search of any account of any image that he had kept in mind while he wrote. And even if I should happen to notice, at some time in the future, on some or another bookshelf in some or another house where I am a visitor, a certain biography of Thomas Hardy or a certain book about so-called madonnas, I should avoid looking into the book for fear of obliterating a mental image that was not a mere copy of details seen long ago on a page of a book but proof of something I had for long wanted to believe, namely, that my mind was the source of not only my wants and desires but the imagery that tempered them.

Since I wrote the previous paragraph, I have travelled to and from the capital city where I lived for most of my life. I travelled there in order to visit my grandson and his parents and the only two friends of mine that I still care to visit. In the house where I stayed for two days and nights, the windows of the three main rooms are bordered with panels of what I intend to call from here on *coloured glass*. (I am so ignorant in these matters that I do not even know whether the terms *stained glass* and *leadlight glass* refer to the same thing, which is to say that I do not know whether the glass in the churches where I sometimes supposed as a boy that to pray was to see on the white of one's soul the rainbow-coloured shafts from the windows of heaven—whether that glass is the same as the glass in the upper panes of the window that overlooked my bed last night and on the preceding night: the window the blind of which I felt compelled to pull up after I had lain down, so that I could learn before I fell asleep how the glow from the street-light outside was changed before it fell on me.) Of course, I had noticed and admired these panes in the past, but during my latest visit to the house I was thinking often of this piece of writing, which had come to an end, for the time being, at the last words of the previous paragraph. I was thinking also of the window in the small church near this house and of the question why the sight of the murky glass in that window had set me writing this report, as I call it. Thinking thus, I looked often at the upper panes as though they might suggest something of meaning.

I had intended to pull down the blind before I fell asleep, but I woke at first light with the bare glass above me. (The window was without curtains.) In the design nearest my face, the coloured pieces seemed meant to represent stems and leaves and petals, but their effect on me was more than should have derived from mere likenesses of parts of plants. I glanced several times at the glass from the sides of my eyes. This way of looking at notable sights has sometimes taught me more than gazing or staring. Then I looked directly at the glass but with eyes almost closed. This had the effect of blurring some of the boundaries between plain and tinted areas, so that the sky outside seemed mottled with pink and pale orange in the same way that the sky had been mottled on certain mornings during my last weeks of secondary school, more than fifty years before. Those were the last few mornings of spring and the first few mornings of summer. My alarm clock woke me before sunrise. The others of my family were still asleep. I washed and dressed quietly and then sat at the kitchen table in such a way that I could see the eastern sky through the window. In front of me were my set texts for the matriculation examination in Latin: the *Agricola* of Tacitus, one of the books of Virgil's *Aeneid*, and Cicero's *De Divinatione*. My class had been badly taught for year after year in Latin. Several of the religious brothers assigned to us in earlier years had seemed to know less Latin than the most able few in our class, of whom I was one. In our second year, we had been assigned a lay-teacher who was a trembling alcoholic unable to learn our names or to write on the blackboard. Our teacher in our final year was competent enough, but by then I had become accustomed to teaching myself. For a few hours each night, I studied my other subjects, in which I was well versed. Then I went to bed early and afterwards rose early to study Latin for two hours while the house and the neighbourhood were quiet. During winter and for much of spring, the sky outside was dark, but during the last weeks before my examinations the sun rose while I sat over my Latin books. By then, I felt confident. I had almost mastered my set texts. Even the most difficult passages in the Virgil were becoming clear to me during the first bright mornings of summer, and while I read and translated with growing elation, the Latin text itself seemed attuned to my mood. The long journey of the Trojan exiles was almost at an end. On a certain morning, even before the sun had risen, the heroes of the poem divined, if not saw, the first hint of their dreamed-of destination.

Iam rubescebat stellis aurora fugatis

This single line of the *Aeneid* sounded several times in my mind while I was writing the previous sentences. I believe the English equivalent of the Latin to be: The stars had now been put to flight, and the dawn was reddening.

I had almost mastered the reading and writing of the Latin language by the early summer of a certain year in the mid-1950s, but today, more than fifty years later, I can recall only that one line from all that I read and wrote in Latin during a period of five years, and I can think of no more worthy task for me at present than that I should set out to discover why this one line stays with me and why sometimes nowadays, here in this border district, four hundred kilometres from the place where I studied Latin on a few summer mornings long ago—why the sight of certain colours in the sky in the early morning will still sometimes cause me to recite with elation:

Iam rubescebat stellis aurora fugatis

As I remember it, the day when the dawn reddened was the day when the Trojans, after years of wandering, had their first sight of their true homeland. In spite of everything, against all odds, the travellers had reached their destination. How could this not have stirred a seventeen-years-old schoolboy, especially when he learned of it through the medium of an epic poem in a language other than his own on one of the last mornings before he himself set out on what he thought of as a journey towards a homeland-of-the-mind; before he put away his textbooks for the last time and became free to read whatever books he chose.

In his second-last year in school, he was placed first in the class in English. He received as his prize a large, single-volume history of English literature chosen for him, he assumed, by his English teacher. This was a religious brother, a man that his prize-winning pupil neither liked nor disliked and seldom thought of in later years except in connection with a certain anecdote that he still remembered in detail fifty-five years later. In one of their first English periods for the year, the brother had warned his class not to be too much influenced by their religious beliefs when answering questions at their final examination. The boys who heard this advice had been taught for years past to be proud of their religion and to miss no opportunity for declaring their beliefs to the world, but they did not find their teacher's advice in this instance strange or unsettling. They knew that the persons marking their papers at public examinations were likely to be high-school teachers or university tutors: persons from the secular system, as the boys would have called it; persons likely to be agnostics at best and atheists at worst, and perhaps even sympathetic to communism.

The anecdote mentioned in the previous paragraph was as follows. The brother, the boys' English teacher, was on the way to completing an Arts degree with a major study in English at the university that was then the only university in the capital city in a suburb of which was the boys' school. (The boys were not all dismayed to learn that their English teacher was less qualified than any comparable teacher in the so-called secular system; the boys understood that their own school received no funds from any government and that their teachers paid for their own training.) The brother had been required, during his second year as a university student of English, to write an essay discussing some or another comment on the poem *Paradise Lost*, by John Milton. Whether or not the brother had discussed the comment, he had taken the opportunity to point out in his essay what seemed to him the most noticeable and the most reprehensible matter to be understood from the poem; he had pointed out that the narrator of the poem, whom he identified as John Milton, was on the side of Satan, or the Devil. The tutor who assessed the brother's essay had awarded it a mark below Pass but had invited the brother to submit an amended version. The brother had then submitted an amended version of his essay and had been awarded a mark within the range of Pass.

When the schoolboy mentioned earlier had first heard this anecdote, he had not felt urged to pass judgement on either the brother or the tutor. The boy knew nothing about the university or what might have taken place there. He had travelled so little that he had never seen so much as a distant view of the university, which was in a suburb far from his own. A few years later, if the young man who had been the schoolboy had recalled the anecdote he would have considered the brother a fool, first because he believed in the reality of a personage that he called Satan or the Devil, second because he felt obliged to preach against any affront to his religious beliefs, and third because he had tried to judge a poem on moral rather than aesthetic grounds. Some years later again, when the man who had been the young man was a part-time student of English at the university he sometimes recalled the anecdote and was of the opinion that the brother ought to have been awarded for the first version of his essay a mark within the range of first-class honours, given that he had reported in that essay his honest, unfeigned experience as a reader, which was something that the man's tutors and lecturers seemed unable or unwilling to do.

Students of English at the university were required to study only a certain number of the list of set texts for each year of the course. The man mentioned previously chose not to study *Paradise Lost* when he found it on such a list. This was not from any reason connected to the anecdote mentioned but because the man was unwilling to read at length about the same mythical beings and events that had occupied his mind during much of his childhood and youth. He had decided as a young man, some years before, that he no longer believed in the reality of those beings and events. If pressed to explain more exactly his loss of belief, the young man might have said that he no longer accepted that certain images in his mind were images of actual beings able to punish or reward him. As a student of English, the man was made weary by the mere thought of his having to read a long work of fiction believed by its author to be a report of actual events, not to mention his afterwards having to find a way of praising the work in words acceptable to his tutor and examiner. The same man also preferred not to call to mind again the images mentioned because they seemed connected with many of the fears and anxieties that had troubled him as a child and a youth. If the man had recalled just then the image of the young woman with the doves at her breasts, he might have felt less reluctant to read *Paradise Lost*, although he would still have dreaded, and rightly so, the task of pretending to respond to the text as his teachers expected him to respond. If the man had recalled the image of the young woman, he might have begun to understand that an image in the mind is itself real, whether or not it may be said to denote some other class of entity; that the dark-haired image-woman standing in the shaft of image-light from the image-window was by then as much a part of him as was any of his bodily organs. He might have begun to understand that even the images that he claimed no longer to believe in—even

37

these were necessary for his salvation, even if they were no more than evidence of his need for saving imagery.

During many weeks of his childhood, his parents borrowed and read two or three books from some or another so-called circulating library in their nearest shopping centre. In the years before television was available in the capital city, a circulating library flourished in every suburban shopping centre. Subscribers to a library borrowed for a modest fee one after another book of a kind sometimes called by publishers *library fiction*. The books had been originally published with hard covers and dust-jackets, but before they were made available for borrowing the dust-jacket of each had been removed by the librarian. She (the proprietor of a circulating library was invariably female) would then have cut from the dust-jacket first the front panel and then the inside panel on which was printed the so-called blurb. These panels she glued to the front and rear cover respectively. She finally brushed over both covers a clear varnish or lacquer. The boy's parents went to bed on most evenings long before he had finished his homework. If he passed their bedroom door, he would see them side by side, propped up on pillows, and each reading by the light of the bedlamp fixed to the bedhead between them one or another of the books with the glazed covers. Sometimes, when both of his parents were out, the boy read as much as a chapter from one or another of the glazed books that lay always in his parents' bedroom or in the lounge-room. Sometimes, when his mother was busy but not far away, he had time for reading only a page or two at the place where her or his father's bookmark rested. What he read thus furtively would surely have reported the thoughts and deeds of a variety of fictional characters in a variety of fictional settings, but he who had been the boy seemed, as from only a few years afterwards, to remember what he had read from the borrowed books as passage after passage or chapter after chapter in one never-ending book. Likewise, the many fictional characters that he had read about he seemed to remember as two only: a young male character and a young female character.

Nearly sixty years after he had first conceived of the never-ending book, the man who had been the boy mentioned above remembered the setting of the book as a far-reaching landscape of pale-green meadows interspersed with patches of dark-green woodland. Each meadow was bordered with flowering hedgerows. In each woodland were paths leading past banks overgrown by wildflowers with appealing names. Here and there in the landscape were large houses of two and more storeys and with numerous chimneys. Each house was surrounded by a spacious formal garden at the far end of which was a park with an ornamental lake. Each large house was occupied for the time being not only by several of the latest generations of the family that had owned the house for several centuries but also by a sort of floating population of youngish men and women who were distant relatives of the owners of the house or who had been recommended to the owners by some or another friend or distant relative in a city that might have been named London and was no more than a conjectured smokey blur far away past the furthest of the pale-green meadows. Each member of this numerous population had been thus recommended because he or she had recently suffered from some or another bereavement or personal crisis. The persons thus recommended were at leisure during the whole of their lengthy stay at the large house. None seemed concerned with earning income and each was in possession of an extensive wardrobe together with tennis racquets, golf clubs, and perhaps even a motor-car.

The remembering man remembered also that the chief concern of the young persons who lived or who were staying as guests in the large houses mentioned was to fall in love with one another. The boy who was long afterwards the remembering man was not at all surprised when he first learned this. Falling in love would have been his own chief concern if ever he had found himself in one of the large houses mentioned in the landscape mentioned. The glimpses of far woodlands, the exquisite greenness of the meadows, the lines of trees concealing shallow streams in the lowest parts of the valleys—this satisfying scenery alone could not have fully satisfied him. He would have had to search among the young female persons of his acquaintance for someone whose image in his mind seemed not averse to his explaining to her how he felt towards such scenery for as long as he was preparing to approach her.

The remembering man could never remember any detail of the appearance in his mind long before of any of the young male or female personages who had fallen in love with one another in what had seemed an endless book. All such details were lost to view in far parts of his mind as from the time during his tenth year when he began to read furtively the first episode of a long work of fiction that was published in serial form in one after another monthly issue of a magazine passed on to his mother by a woman-neighbour who could afford to buy the magazine, which was published in England, so the remembering man remembered, although he had forgotten its title and the appearance of its front cover. The man could never recall himself studying the details of any of the duotone illustrations that appeared each month on the first of the pages where the fictional text appeared. He could not even recall any detail of any face in the illustrations. Yet the man had clearly in mind while I was composing this sentence a certain image of a young woman with dark hair and a wistful expression and of a young man with a troubled expression. Whenever afterwards he tried to recall any of the image-fallers-in-love who had appeared to him while he was reading the many pages of fiction that he had read as a boy, these were the only two that he recalled.

A young Englishwoman is travelling by ocean-liner from London to Ceylon in one of the first years after the Second World War. She is going to Ceylon in order to be married to a tea-planter, the owner of a large estate. Soon after leaving London, the young woman meets up with a young man who is also travelling to Ceylon. The man is a journalist on his way to take up an appointment with a leading newspaper there. Or, perhaps he is a writer of fiction on his way to research the background of his next book. The two young persons dance together and later talk together on deck. On subsequent days they meet and talk often. Even the nine-years-old boy-reader of the text in which these matters are reported—even he soon understands that the young woman finds the young man more lively and more interesting than her fiancé, who has begun to seem stolid in comparison. Once having understood this, the boy-reader changes his allegiance. Previously, he had felt in sympathy with the man on the liner who had met up with a desirable young woman who was already bespoken. Previously, the boy-reader could foresee nothing better for the man on the liner than that he should return soon to England, there to mingle with the other young persons of his kind in the fictional green landscape described earlier, where he would be more likely than in a sweltering country with dark-skinned inhabitants to meet up with a young woman of pale complexion who was still unattached. Now, however, when the events of the narrative were falling in favour of the man on the liner, the boy-reader began to transfer his sympathy to the tea-planter, the man sitting alone on the veranda of his bungalow among the mountains and not suspecting that his long-awaited wife-to-be was preparing to break their engagement. The boy-reader prepared to share the man's heavy-heartedness after he had learned his fate and to hope that he would soon sell off his plantation and return to England, there to mingle with the other young persons of his kind as his rival in love might previously have been expected to do.

Anyone reading this report would be surely able to anticipate the outcome of the fictional events summarised above: the shipboard romance, so to call it, going forward; the young woman's seeming more and more to accept that she had fallen in love with her new suitor and ought to break her engagement; then the narrative's taking an unexpected turn, after which the young woman comes to decide that the charm and the glamour of the man on the liner are in some way deceptive and not to be compared with the sincerity and trustworthiness of the man waiting for her on his plantation. In fact, the remembering man remembered nothing whatever of the ending, although he never doubted that the young woman remained true to her tea-planter—even in his tenth year, he had learned many of the conventions of so-called romance fiction. I am not concerned here to report the passing thoughts of the boy while he read in haste from some or another women's magazine that his mother had left lying about. What interests me is a man's having kept in mind for more than sixty years an image of a female face and even of a certain expression on that face, which images first occurred to him while he was reading a work of fiction every detail of which was surely forgotten long ago by every other reader of the work. (An image of a male face also stayed in mind, but mostly as a means used sometimes by the rememberer when he supposed that he might feel more keenly as a fictional tea-planter or a fictional male passenger on an ocean-liner than as a rememberer of an image-face.) What interests me also is the man's seeming to have assumed during most of his life that the image-female whose face he kept in mind was above reproach or blame; that any seeming fault in her character was no more than an endearing imperfection. If, for the fictional time being, she was a young woman on an ocean-liner seeming to encourage a certain suitor while she was betrothed to another man, she was neither capricious nor indecisive, much less disloyal, and male characters and male readers alike were obliged to accept her changes of feeling and to abide by her choices. What interests me finally is that neither the boy nor the man ever looked forward to

treating in the so-called real world with some or another like-
ness or counterpart of any of the image-heroines who appeared to them while they read certain works of fiction. Both
the boy and the man were attracted often to some or another female face resembling that of his fictional girlfriend or
wife, but what followed more resembled the rapid reading to
its end of a work of fiction than a courtship or an attempted
seduction.

More than thirty years ago, I copied in longhand from the
major work of fiction by Marcel Proust a passage purporting
to explain why the bond between reader and fictional character is closer than any bond between flesh-and-blood persons. I
put the statement among my files, but I failed to find it just
now after having searched for it for nearly an hour. I first copied the statement because I could not understand it. I understood the matter that Proust was trying to explain but I could
not understand his explanation. I filed the statement in the
hope that I could later study it until I was able to understand
it. Today, while I was writing the previous paragraphs, I seemed
to arrive at my own explanation for the intimacy between a
reading boy and a remembering man on the one hand and on
the other hand a female personage brought into being by passages of fiction. (I do not consider the boy and the man fictional
characters. I am not writing a work of fiction but a report of
seemingly fictional matters.) I then felt urged to look again at
the statement by Marcel Proust so that I could first try again
to understand it and could then compare Marcel Proust's explanation with my own. I will look again in future for the statement, but in the meanwhile I am not at all put out. Marcel

Proust may have had his explanation, but I now have my own explanation.

I seem to remember Marcel Proust's having written that the author of fiction was able so to report the feelings of a fictional character that the reader was able to feel closer to that character than to any living person. Did I read the word *feelings* in the English translation that I read long ago? And, if I did so read, was that word the nearest English equivalent of the French word used by Marcel Proust for the precious item that the writer of fiction reported to the reader? In earlier years, I would have striven to answer these questions. Today, I content myself with my own formulation of the matter: sometimes, while reading a work of fiction, I seem to have knowledge of what it would be to have knowledge of the essence of some or another personality. If asked to explain the meaning of the word *essence* in the previous sentence, I would do so by referring to the part of myself (the seeming part of my seeming self?) that apprehends (seems to apprehend?) the knowledge (seeming knowledge?) mentioned in the previous sentence.

After I had written the previous paragraph, I succeeded in finding among my files a statement that I copied more than thirty years ago from a biography of George Gissing. "What a farce is Biography," George Gissing once wrote in a letter. "The only true biographies are to be found in novels."

The whole of the rear page of the dust-jacket of my copy of a certain biography of George Gissing is given over to a reproduction of a black and white photograph of the young female author of the book. She was photographed in profile. She chose, or she was directed, to stand side-on to the camera.

It is not possible to tell from the vagueness surrounding her whether she posed indoors or outdoors; behind her is a wall of bricks or stones; in the background is another wall forming a right angle with the first; in the second wall is what seems at first glance a doorway leading to a brightly lit further room or out into bright daylight but may be no more than a rectangular patch of light reflected from some or another window or mirror beyond the range of the camera. Whenever I pick up the book and look anew at the rear of the dust-jacket, my eye is led at first to the seeming doorway but an instant later to an equally noticeable lighted area in the upper foreground. The author stares intently while a bright source from somewhere ahead of her forms zones of light on a part of her forehead, on her nearer cheekbone, on her chin, on the ridge of her nose, and on the cornea of her nearer eye. (Her further eye is hidden from view.) The author's face might not have taken my attention if I had first seen it lit evenly by daylight or electric light, but the image of her face in the reproduction of the photograph on the dust-jacket of her biography of George Gissing—that image has remained with me during the thirty or more years since I first bought the book and stored it on my shelves. I read the book itself in the year after I had bought it, but often in the following years I took the book down from its shelf and stared at the rear page of the dust-jacket. I stared sometimes at the background, and especially at the rectangular patch of light, trying to learn what sort of place the young woman had been posed in or had insisted on posing in. Mostly, however, I stared at the image of the young woman.

I stared because I felt as though something of value might

appear to me as a result of my staring. I tried to stare at the image of the face of the young woman with the same intense stare that the original young woman had once directed at something visible, or perhaps invisible, on the far side of the light that picked out the prominences of her face. I tried to stare as though something of meaning might appear to me if only I could turn aside from, or see beyond, all extraneous objects of sight; if only I could see truly and without distraction. After I had failed to see what I had hoped to see, I allowed my eyes to pass again from lighted patch to lighted patch and to rest at last on the most arresting detail of all: the filament of darkness or shade enclosed within two semi-circles of light, all of which together represented the cornea and iris of the right eye of the young woman as it appeared at the instant when she was photographed with the bright light directed at her. Sometimes, the bright semi-circles at the front of her eye brought to my mind a theory of vision that was given credence in some or another earlier age. (If no such theory was ever given credence, then I dreamed of having read about it, but the theory, whether actual or dreamed, remains relevant to this passage of writing.) According to the theory, a person perceives an object of sight by means of a ray of light emitted through the eye of a person. The ray travels outwards from the eye and then renders visible the object of sight. If I subscribed to this theory, I would probably suppose that the young biographer had been photographed just at the moment when her eye lighted on an object of much interest to her: perhaps an object visible only to her.

Hardly any details of the young woman's life are reported

on the dust-jacket of her biography of George Gissing. I am therefore unable to think of her as recalling so-called scenes from the past or day-dreaming about some or another future. I know her only as the biographer of George Gissing and, according to the dust-jacket of the first edition of her biography of him, the author of five books of fiction. And so, whenever she seems to me to be looking blankly ahead I think of her mental imagery as deriving from one or another of the five works of fiction that she wrote while her eyes were similarly averted from what is commonly called the world or as deriving from one or another of the many works of fiction written by a man who died about forty years before she was born; I think of her as contemplating essences of personages.

I wrote the two previous paragraphs while the book mentioned was in its usual place on my shelves. After I had written the phrase *essences of personages* just now, I was prompted to retrieve the book and to place it here beside me with the rear of the dust-jacket uppermost. My eye was then led on its usual route from the rectangular zone of light towards the source of light outside the boundaries of the illustration, then back towards the highlighted features of the young woman staring ahead of her, and finally to the surface of her nearer eye. Now, however, and for whatever reason, that seeming object of my vision seems other than a representation of a human eye. Now, I am able to disregard for an instant the surrounding zones of darkness and light—the representations of part of a human face—and to make out of three mere blotches and stripes, two of white surrounding one of dark grey, an image of a whole and perfectly formed glass marble. When the instant has passed, the surrounding zones, as I called them, come back into my view but the seeming glass marble remains at their centre. What I seem then to see is no grotesquerie—a young woman with a globe of coloured glass for an eye—but what is surely an anatomical impossibility: a young woman holding a glass marble firmly between upper and lower eyelid at the front of a normal eye. The presence there of the glass marble might well explain the peculiar intensity of the young woman's stare. Before I first saw, as it were, the glass marble resting against the eye, I was at a loss to explain why the young woman had often the look of someone staring intently at something visible only to her: something that seemed to hang in the middle distance before her although it existed nowhere but in her mind. How, I wondered, was the young woman able to keep her attention fixed thus while she posed in front of a camera and among bright sources of light? If she held a sphere of coloured glass against her eyeball, all is explained.

While I could never bear to have a glass marble, or any other object, resting against the surface of my eye, I held often, as a child, one after another marble as near as I dared to my open left eye while I peered into the glass. I looked always towards a source of strong light—an electric globe or a sunlit sky—and the sort of marble I looked into was always translucent. The marble that I envisage as resting against the eyeball of the biographer of George Gissing—that marble is not of the kind that I looked into as a child. The marble that the young woman looks into or through is of a kind containing a dense, richly coloured core surrounded by transparent glass. The core is usually of one or another primary colour. When I began to collect glass marbles in the 1940s, this kind of marble was one of the least-valued of the many kinds passed from hand to hand among my schoolfellows. We collectors of marbles hoarded older kinds passed on to us by fathers or uncles and no longer sold in shops. I preferred the older kinds not only for their scarcity but for their being mostly of translucent or murky glass with skeins or whorls of a second colour deep inside the predominant colour. Marbles of these kinds did not readily give their contents away.

I was at first disappointed after I had seemed to see resting against the young woman's eye a glass marble that I valued little as a child: a sort sold cheaply in Coles stores and having nothing more mysterious for its contents than a simple core of white or red or blue or yellow or green. Later, I looked for the first time in many years at the hundred and more glass marbles that I have kept by me during six decades and despite my having lived at nearly twenty addresses. I tumbled the marbles out from the glass jars their containers and onto the carpet near my desk. I wanted to find among the pebs and agates and cat's-eyes and pearlies and realies and others the few of the kind that I now thought of as *eyeballs*. I hoped to learn that I had been wrong to dismiss their kind: that the simple appearance of the eyeballs had been deceptive. The glass jars contained not only glass marbles. There lay on the carpet among my former playthings a silver-coloured tube as long as a cigarette but somewhat thicker. I had forgotten my having acquired, perhaps twenty years before, the first kaleidoscope that I had seen. For much of my life, I had read references to kaleidoscopes. I may even sometimes have used the words *kaleidoscope* or *kaleidoscopic* in speech or writing. I understood a kaleidoscope to be a toy that produced constantly changing patterns. But I had never seen or handled a kaleidoscope until the wife of a certain friend of mine presented me with the silver-coloured tube mentioned earlier. She and her husband had been travelling in the United States of America and had noticed in the city of Roanoke, Virginia, a shop selling only kaleidoscopes, the largest being of the size of a small tree-trunk. My friend's wife, in whose company I had always felt less than comfortable, told me while she handed me the small kaleidoscope that she had thought of me as soon as she had seen the window-display in Roanoke. I was puzzled by her statement, but she did not elaborate and I did not want to give her the satisfaction of believing that she knew something about me that I myself was unaware of.

Even before I had taken the kaleidoscope from the woman, I got a mild pleasure from knowing that the thing, whatever its uses and its benefits might have been, had come from the state of Virginia. The word *Virginia* denotes a small coloured area in the widespread terrain of my mind. In the foreground of this area is an expanse of pale green; in the background is a line or ridge of dark blue. The pale green is intersected by dark-green stripes and studded by dark-green blotches. In a few of the pale-green areas are roughly elliptical shapes outlined in white and marked in places by bars of dark green. My image, so to call it, of the state of Virginia derives from my happening to have read, many years ago, that the residents of some or another district of the state affected some of the ways of the English upper classes: planting hedgerows between their

51

fields, riding to hounds, and conducting steeplechases on their racecourses. Nothing else that I might have read about Virginia has altered this image.

Surely my image-Virginia appeared to me for a moment while my friend's wife was presenting me with my kaleidoscope and while I was putting on a show of gratitude and preparing to look through the instrument, but surely I also failed at the time to notice that my mental scenery, so to call it, was not an integral landscape but an assortment of image-fragments not unlike those brought into view by means of a kaleidoscope. (While I was writing the previous sentence, I wondered how soon after the events there reported did I discover how much of what I was used to calling *thinking* or *remembering* or *imagining* was no more than my bringing into the range of my mental vision such coloured shapes and fragments as those behind the place-name *Virginia*.) The thing presented to me in the west-facing room that was my family's and my lounge-room and also the room where many of my books were shelved—the thing was not merely a tube for looking into. At one end, a sickle-shaped piece of wire was attached to the metal casing of the tube. The purpose of the wire was to hold a glass marble in place at the end of the tube, and just such a marble was in place when I took possession of the instrument. (I have since learned that some kaleidoscopes consist of a tube that is rotated by the person using it and contains the pieces of coloured glass that form the various patterns appearing to the user. The tube that I was given remained fixed while the user turned this way and that the glass marble resting against the further end of the tube.)

When I first saw the glass marble at the end of my kaleidoscope, I had been for at least ten years the owner of the above-mentioned biography of George Gissing. I had read the book once through and had sometimes afterwards looked into it. On the afternoon when I took possession of the kaleidoscope, the book would have been standing among rows of other books on one or another of the shelves of books on the east wall of the west-facing room. When I first held my kaleidoscope up to my left eye and turned my face towards the window, certain rays of the same sunlight that passed through the glass marble and then through the metal tube towards my eye would have travelled past my face and then across the room and would then have reached the book mentioned. The rear of the dust-jacket of the book would have been out of view and resting against the front of the dust-jacket of the neighbouring book, which was probably one or another work of fiction by George Gissing. During the moments while I turned the glass marble in its sickle-shaped holder and while I held the other end of the metal tube to my eye, I would have been aware only of what reached my eye and unaware of the presence behind me of the rows of books on their shelves. Today, however, while I write these words, I am unable to recall, let alone to report, what I saw while I looked down the tube and through the glass marble and into the afternoon sunlight. This is a result of my having recalled a few days ago, while I was reporting on a previous page the details of the illustration on the rear of the dust-jacket mentioned often, the precise colour of the translucent core of the mostly transparent glass marble resting against the end of the kaleidoscope.

Until I began writing the previous paragraph, I had never considered strange the fact that I had looked during my lifetime at many thousands of so-called black and white illustrations or photographic prints or the like without seeming to observe, let alone regret, that the persons or places or things represented were without colour. (I can call to mind at present only one instance of my seeming to see coloured details in an illustration lacking them. This instance was reported earlier in these pages.) While I was writing the previous paragraph, however, I seemed to see, in a zone of colourless space adjoining a black and white representation of a human eye, a coloured representation of a glass marble consisting of several whorled membranes of translucent green at the centre of an otherwise transparent globe. A few moments afterwards, I became aware that I had given the name *ice-green* to the colour of the vanes in the glass marble mentioned, which colour was also the colour of the vanes in the glass marble resting against the end of the kaleidoscope that I first looked into on an afternoon of bright sunlight while a certain illustration rested behind me and out of sight on some or another shelf of books. While I was writing the previous sentence, the term *ice-maiden* occurred to me as though it had lain out of sight in my mind since I read it long ago in some or another text of little consequence but as though it now denotes something of relevance to this report.

I consider myself a student of colours and shades and hues and tints. *Crimson lake, burnt umber, ultramarine . . .* I was too clumsy as a child to paint with my moistened brush the scenery that I would have liked to bring into being. I preferred to leave untouched in their white metallic surroundings my rows of powdery rectangles of water-colours, to read aloud one after another of the tiny printed names of the coloured rectangles, and to let each colour seem to soak into each word of its name or even into each syllable of each word of each name so that I could afterwards call to mind an exact shade or hue from an image of no more than black letters on a white ground.

Deep cadmium, geranium lake, imperial purple, parchment . . . after the last of our children had found employment and had moved out of our home, my wife and I were able to buy for ourselves things that had previously been beyond our means. I bought my first such luxury, as I called it, in a shop selling artists' supplies. I bought there a complete set of coloured pencils made by a famous maker of pencils in England: a hundred and twenty pencils, each stamped with gold lettering along its side and having at its end a perfectly tapered wick. The collection of pencils is behind me as I write these words. It rests near the jars of glass marbles and the kaleidoscope mentioned earlier. None of the pencils has ever been used in the way that most pencils are used, but I have sometimes used the many-striped collection in order to confirm my suspicion as a child that each of what I called my long-lost moods might be recollected and, perhaps, preserved if only I could look again at the precise shade or hue that had become connected with the mood—that had absorbed, as it were, or had been permeated with, one or more of the indefinable qualities that constitute what is called a mood or a state of feeling. During the weeks since I first wrote in the earlier pages of this report about the windows in the church of white stone, I have spent every day an increasing amount of time in moving my pencils to and fro among the hollow spaces allotted to them in their container. I seem to recall that I tried sometimes, many years ago, to move my glass marbles from place to place on the carpet near my desk with the vague hope that some or another chance arrangement of them would restore to me some previously irretrievable mood. The marbles, however, were too variously coloured, and each differed too markedly from the other. Their colours seemed to vie, to compete. Or, a single marble might suggest more than I was in search of: a whole afternoon in my childhood or a row of trees in a backyard when I had wanted back only a certain few moments when my face was brushed by a certain few leaves. Among the pencils are many differing only subtly from their neighbours. Six at least I might have called simply *red* if I had not learned long ago their true names. With these six, and with still others from each side of them, I often arrange one after another of many possible sequences, hoping to see in the conjectured space between some or another unlikely pair a certain tint that I have wanted for long to see.

On a certain morning nearly sixty years ago, when the sun was shining through the window of the kitchen where my mother had set me to wash and dry the breakfast dishes, I heard from the radio on the mantelpiece above the fireplace the distinctive, harsh-sounding voice of a man who seemed sometimes to sing and sometimes to narrate, all the while accompanying himself on a piano. What he sang about or narrated was his having once, long before, caused by chance a certain chord to sound while he sat at the piano fingering the keys; his having been strangely affected by the sound of the chord; and his having tried in vain during many years since to find again the combination of notes that had caused the chord to sound. I knew hardly more then than I know now about popular music and those who perform it, but I understood that the man with the harsh voice was a comic and I was even aware that his song was a humorous version of a song performed in music halls and parlours long before my birth. (I happened to have read a reference to this song in a book of comic strips with the title *Radio Fun Annual*, which had been a Christmas present ten years before from my mother, who could not have known that the characters and the settings in the comic strips all derived from radio programs in England, so that the references in the comic strips mostly baffled me.)

I readily understood, on that morning nearly sixty years ago, that a person might lament the loss of some or another musical sound last heard many years before. I myself valued certain passages of popular music, not for themselves but as a means of restoring to me certain combinations of feelings. If only I were resourceful enough to find and to play some or another electronic recording of a certain recitative by a long-dead American performer and of his dissonant thumpings on a piano, then I might discover again, after nearly sixty years, what seems today one of my own lost mental chords but would have seemed at the time a mere longing for something soon to be recovered. While I stood at the kitchen sink in my parents' house in the 1950s, I was likely to have been trying not to hear a lost chord but to see such as the precise shade of red that I had seen ten years before on the leaves of an ornamental grape-vine near the panels of frosted glass in the wall of the garage at one side of a certain large house. The garage and the house were of brick or of stone covered with cream-coloured stucco. They stood in a spacious garden in a suburb of a provincial city in the north of the state the western border of which lies fifty kilometres from where I sit writing about the leaves of the grape-vine that I last saw sixty-five years ago on the first evening after my parents and my younger brother and I had travelled by train from the capital city and across the Great Dividing Range to the provincial city where we were going to live thenceforth.

I had never previously travelled north of the capital city, and I was surprised by the heat of the air beyond the Great Divide and by the glare of the sunlight in the footpaths of the suburbs of the provincial city, which footpaths were of gravel that was mostly white with strands of a shade of orange-yellow that I supposed at first were traces of the gold that had made the city famous. Our furniture would not arrive until the following day. We were to spend the night in spare rooms in the cream-coloured house with the spacious garden. In the early evening, when the air was still hot, I walked alone into the garden. I was not a timid child but I was scrupulously obedient. I wanted to impress adults so that they would see me as more than a mere child: as someone worthy to converse with them and even, perhaps, worthy to be instructed in some of the secret lore of adults. I kept to the paths in the garden. I would have liked to inspect the clearings between the shrubs on the lawn or the summer-house with walls of dark-green lattice and pots of ferns visible through the doorway, but I chose to consider those places out of bounds, and I hoped my avoiding them would persuade anyone secretly observing me that I was mature and trustworthy.

On the shaded side of the house, I stopped when a cement path gave way to flagstones set at intervals in soil where tufts of moss survived even in summer. The place ahead of me was bounded on one side by part of the cream-coloured southern wall of the house. The one window overlooking the place was almost filled with the satiny flounces of a certain curtain or blind that I would recall in later years whenever I came across such phrases as *luxurious mansion* or *sumptuous furnishings*. On the opposite boundary, which was the southern boundary of the property, the leaves of an ornamental grape-vine were beginning to redden. Much of the space ahead of me was overgrown with irises and ferns, but I could see among the greenery areas of murky water where broad floating leaves surely concealed red-gold fish. Opposite where I stood, the far boundary of the place was a many-paned wall of frosted glass that I learned long afterwards was the rear wall of the garage, although it seemed to me at first sight part of an enclosed veranda where one or another female occupant of the house would lie on a cane lounge with a book in her hands during the hottest hours of many an afternoon.

While I stood on the last section of the cement path, I thought of the place ahead as having been designed for the exclusive enjoyment of privileged persons unknown to me but almost certainly female. And yet the place was part of a garden and was marked off by no barrier. Its stern female proprietors had surely allowed for the possibility that more than one curious visitor, even an ignorant male child such as I, would approach the place from time to time and might even decide, in his ignorance, that he was free to enter.

My speculations led me to no decision. I thought of falling back on the ploy that had sometimes seemed to keep adults from suspecting that I spied on them. I thought of stepping into the place ahead and, if I was later challenged or questioned, of playing the part of the guileless child who wanted no more than to look into a far corner of a mere garden: a child who saw only surfaces and was never driven to learn their connotations.

In the event, no decision was required of me. A tall girl, almost a young woman, stepped from behind me, took my hand, and led me forward, treading lightly on the mossy ground so that I could walk on the flagstones. I supposed her to be the daughter of the household, the only child of her parents. I had not previously seen her. When my family had arrived at the house, she was in her room with the door closed—studying, so we were told. While she led me towards the shaded pond, I had still not looked her in the face; I had learned from a sidelong glance only that the skin around her cheekbone had a sort of lustre and that she looked at things intently.

She seemed to have supposed that I was curious to see the fishpond but afraid of trampling the plants surrounding it. I said nothing to prevent her from thinking she was correct. I stood where she directed me to stand, and I found the words to persuade her that the sight of the scarlet fish in the dark-green water was the reward I had hoped for when she first took my hand. How could I have begun to tell what I truly felt when even today, more than sixty years later, I labour over these sentences, trying to report what was more an intimation of a state of mind than an actual experience? I was pleased and flattered to be in the company of the girl-woman, and yet I wished she had asked me to give an account of myself before she led me in among the ferns and the irises. As grateful as I was for her patronage, I wished she could have been made to understand that I had hoped for more than could be disclosed to me even in that pleasant place and even with her as my guide.

Later on that same day, the mother of the girl-woman took me to a room that she called her sewing-room. While I watched, she sewed on her treadle-driven machine a small cloth bag with draw-strings at the top. Then, while I held open the bag, she poured into it from her cupped hands more than twenty glass marbles that she had taken from a vase of a stuff that I knew as crystal in a piece of furniture that I knew as a crystal cabinet the doors of which comprised many small panes of glass, some of them frosted. I was told by the woman that the bag was a reward. I supposed her daughter had spoken of me favourably, and I longed to know what about me had so impressed her.

I had never owned any marbles, although I had seen and admired many in the possession of older boys. Those given me by the woman became the foundation of my own collection, and many of them remain with me today. If this piece of writing were a work of fiction, I might report hereabouts that one of the most prized of my first marbles is of translucent glass

of a shade of red such that whenever I hold the marble between my eye and a source of bright light, I seem to recall the
colour of the leaves on the ornamental grape-vine mentioned
earlier and some at least of what I felt while I stood at the
place where the path ended and before the tall girl, almost a
young woman, led me into the place that had seemed to give
rise to my feelings. Or, I might likewise have reported that another marble that I have owned for more than sixty years is of
mostly transparent glass with a core consisting of several coloured vanes radiating outwards from a central axis. These
vanes are of a shade of green such that when I rotate the marble
slowly at the end of my small kaleidoscope the most predominant of the shades in the symmetrical patterns thus produced
brings to mind the term *ice-green.*

After having written the previous paragraph, I spent several days in the suburbs of the capital city where I lived for
most of my life. I travelled there and back by car. For more
than nine hours, I was alone with empty-seeming countryside
around me. I listened occasionally to a radio broadcast of some
or another horse-race, but for most of the time I travelled in
silence except for the sound of the tyres on the road and of the
air swirling around the car.

For some years before I moved to this district, I used to
spend occasional weekends here. During the hours while I
drove from the capital city to this township and back again,
I tried to observe as much as possible of my surroundings.
I hoped that my constantly glancing at the countryside, especially the long views available from hilltops and plateaus, would
enable me later to arrange in my mind an approximation of a

topographical map of the terrain between the city where I had lived for nearly sixty years and the township where I intended to spend the last years of my life. I might have enjoyed my task if I had not been interrupted by one after another signpost bearing the name of some or another place further off or of a road leading away from the highway. Words, so it seemed, attracted me more than scenery. When I might have been fixing in my mind a view of park-like grazing paddocks and distant forested mountains, I was instead following a chain of thoughts leading away from a mere inscription in black paint on a white signboard. I was, for example, first noting a word that I had for long supposed was a Scottish place-name although I had never found the word in even the most detailed gazetteer of the British Isles; then seeming to recall that the word had been used each winter during my youth by the principal racing club in this state as the name of a certain handicap race; then supposing that the word had been thus used because it was the name of an extensive grazing property owned by a long-serving member of the committee of the racing club, on a part of which property were stabled thoroughbred horses, some of them the winners of famous races; then recalling and afterwards uttering aloud one after another of the nine surnames that I could recall of families of long standing who had owned during my youth extensive properties in the countryside, mostly in the western part of the state— uttering aloud not only each surname but following it the details of the racing colours of each family. While I recited thus, I seemed to see surnames and sets of colours superimposed on a much simplified topographical map: on a river-valley among forested mountains far east of the capital city the surname G—— beneath a pink jacket with a white band; on plains beyond the river-border in the north of the state the surname C—— below a black jacket with a blue sash; on foothills of the Great Dividing Range north of the capital city the surname C—— below a pink jacket with black sleeves and cap; on plains now largely covered by suburbs west of the capital city the surname C—— below a blue jacket and sleeves with a black cap; on much more extensive plains much further to the west the surname M—— beneath a white jacket and sleeves with orange braces, collar, and armbands, all edged in black, and an orange cap; on a plateau forming part of the Great Dividing Range north-west of the capital city the surname F—— beneath a jacket and sleeves marked with blue and white squares and a white cap; in the south-west of the state, among lakes and extinct volcanoes, the surname M—— beneath a yellow jacket with cardinal sleeves and cap; in the far south-west of the state the surname A—— beneath a black jacket with a red band and armbands and a red cap; and, at the end of a road branching away from a highway and superimposed on my mental image of the property with the name that I often read on a signpost, the surname T—— beneath a cream jacket with blue sleeves and cap. Often, after I had recited and seen thus, I carried out a similar exercise with a mental image of a topographical map of England, although several of the family names occurring to me were unconnected with any place-name, which led me, for some or another reason, to see names and colours as hovering near the Scottish or the Welsh border. Among the names and colours that I caused to appear to me were those of Lord D—— (black jacket, white cap); Lord H—— de W—— (jacket, sleeves, and cap all of apricot and described in racebooks and elsewhere by the single word *Apricot*); the Duke of N—— (sky-blue jacket and sleeves with a sky-blue and scarlet quartered cap); the Duke of R—— and G—— (yellow jacket and sleeves with a cap of scarlet velvet); the Duke of N—— (Old Gold); and the Duke of D—— (Straw). After I had called to mind each image-jacket and image-cap from image-England, I tried to hold the image in my mind in the hope of enjoying the peculiar pleasure that I sometimes derived from such images, especially those able to be described by a single word. The pleasure consisted partly of a certain awe or admiration and partly of a certain hopefulness. I had never been interested in the ways of the English aristocracy. I had never even cared to learn the differences between dukes and earls and lords and their like. But I felt drawn to admire any person who could rely on a single colour or shade to represent him and his family. I knew something of heraldry. I had studied in colour plates in books numerous images of coats-of-arms. But none of those complex patterns had affected me as did the assertion by some or another so-called aristocrat that he needed no chevron or fess nor any quarterings of gules or vert or argent; that he declared himself to the world by means of one colour only; that he challenged any inquirer into the nuances and subtleties of his character or his preferences or his history to read those matters from a jacket and a pair of sleeves and a cap of defiant simplicity. The hopefulness that was part of the pleasure mentioned earlier arose from my daring to suppose that I myself might one day light upon one or another shade or hue that would declare to the world as much as I cared to declare of my own invisible attributes. One further strand of the pleasure mentioned arose from my recalling the only detail that had stayed with me from my having read, thirty and more years before, a bulky biography of the writer D. H. Lawrence. As I recalled the matter, someone once asked Lawrence how he supposed persons might occupy themselves if ever they had succeeded, as Lawrence hoped they would succeed, in tearing down the factories and the counting-houses where they presently wasted away their lives. Lawrence replied that the men thus set free to fulfil themselves would first build each a house for himself, would then carve the furniture needed for the house, and would afterwards devote himself to designing and painting emblems of himself.

Or, perhaps, long before I had reached the end of the sequence of thoughts reported above, I saw on a signpost, before the abbreviation *Rd*, a rare surname. A priest of that name had officiated, more than forty years before, at the wedding of one of my wife's woman-friends. The number of guests was not large, and the wedding reception was held at the home of the bride's parents in an inner eastern suburb of the capital city. The bride's father was a wealthy businessman, and the house was of cream-coloured stone, substantial, and surrounded by a spacious garden. I ate and drank with the other guests until a certain time in mid-afternoon. I then stepped into the wide central passage of the house and walked towards the front door. I was on my way to fetch a transistor radio from my car so that I could listen to a broadcast description of a famous horse-race soon to be run in a neighbouring suburb. Long before I had reached the front door, I noticed on either side of the door a tall pane of what I would have called stained glass. The zones of various colours formed what I would have called an abstract pattern, although I seemed to see in it resemblances of leaves and stems and tendrils. (I had entered through the front door earlier without noticing the glass, but by now the front veranda was in sunshine while the light inside the house was subdued.) I stopped for only a moment inside the door, not wanting to attract the notice of anyone in the passage behind me, but the sight of the coloured panes against the sunlight had already changed my mood. As much as I wanted to learn the outcome of the famous race, I felt as though something of importance might be revealed to me if I left my radio where it was and remained on the veranda, keeping the coloured glass at the edge of my field of vision and observing the series of mental images and states of feeling that seemed likely to occur to me.

I strolled the length of the veranda and found that it continued along one side of the house. This only heightened my sense of expectancy. A distant sight of a return veranda, as I had heard it called, had sometimes affected me rather as a pane of coloured glass never failed to do. A cane chair stood on the side section of the veranda. I carried the chair to the corner of the veranda and sat down. On a Saturday afternoon in the 1960s, the sound of motor traffic could hardly be heard in the lesser streets of the capital city. The garden around the house of cream-coloured stone was so dense and the cypress hedge at the front was so tall that I could easily suppose myself to be surrounded not by suburbs but by mostly level cattle- or sheep-country marked only by the dark lines of distant cypress plantations or an isolated clump of trees surrounding a homestead and outbuildings. Even then, more than forty years ago, such scenery often appeared near what seemed to me the western border of my mind. For as long as I lived in the capital city, I was reassured by the sight of these mental grasslands. (When I moved here to live, I did not fail to notice that my route led me from one side to the other of a broad zone of actual grasslands. And yet even in this district the same plains still appear in the west of my mind and would do so no less surely, I suspect, even if I were to move across the border.) During the two minutes and more while the famous horse-race would have been under way in the neighbouring suburb, and while I sat in the cane chair at the corner of the veranda, hearing only the faint sounds of voices from inside the house and watching in my mind one after another possible outcome of the famous race, with one after another set of racing colours foremost, I might have been, so I understood afterwards, the owner of a vast cattle- or sheep-property in the sort of countryside that I would see from the sides of my eyes more than forty years later whenever I travelled between the capital city and the border district where I would finally have settled and whenever I passed a signpost bearing a name that I supposed was a Scottish place-name. The man that I might have been, so I understood afterwards, was the owner of one of the horses contesting a famous race in the capital city. He had been free to travel to the capital city and to watch the famous race but he had chosen to listen to a radio broadcast of the race while he sat on the veranda of his homestead. Perhaps, if the man lived during the decades before horse-races were described in radio broadcasts, he would learn the result of the race only by telephone later in the day. While the man that I might have been sat in sight of the paddocks where his horse had been bred, he might have understood what I could not have put into words as I sat on the veranda of the house of cream-coloured stone feeling as though the conjectured might be sometimes more preferable to the actual or as though renunciation might be sometimes preferable to experience.

Before I went back to the wedding reception, I recalled a quotation that I had read recently from the writer Franz Kafka to the effect that a person might learn all that was needed for salvation without leaving his or her own room. Keep to your room for long enough, and the world will find its way to you and will writhe on the floor in front of you—this was my re-membered version of the quotation, and I got from it on that afternoon the promise that I need only pass in my mind through some or another doorway framed by coloured panes and to wait on some or another shaded veranda in my mind until I should have sight of the finish of race after famous race in the mind of man after man in one after another mostly level dis-trict of what I would recognise, late in life, as the setting of the only mythology of value to me.

While I was still outside the house in the inner eastern sub-urb, I began to fear that I would later be unable to recall in detail my experience on the return veranda, much less the re-assurance that it brought me. (I was a young man, not yet thirty years of age, who would not learn for many years that he could not help but remember most of what he might later have need of.) The time of the year was mid-October. I knew little about garden-plants, but I had noticed as a boy that wisteria was usually in bloom when was run the famous horse-race mentioned in the previous paragraphs. Bunches of mauve wisteria blossom hung along the veranda where I had been sitting. I broke off a small bunch and put it into the pocket of my jacket. I seemed to recall that female characters in fiction set in earlier times had sometimes pressed flowers between the pages of books. I intended to ask my wife later to help me preserve the coloured petals, but I was drunk when we reached home and I put away my suit without remembering the wisteria. Weeks later, while I was dressing for a race-meeting, I found in the pocket of my jacket the shrivelled brown remnants of what had been mauve petals.

I reported in the above paragraphs some of what used to occur to me on my former journeys between the capital city and this district near the border. Last week, I visited the capital city for the second time since my arrival in this district. In keeping with the resolution reported in the very first sentence of this piece of writing, I tried to guard my eyes during the journey. Of course, I had to be alert to my surroundings while driving, but I avoided reading the words on signposts pointing towards places out of sight, and I even tried not to take in the many views of far-reaching countryside that had so often appealed to me. I was still aware of signals from the edges of my field of vision, but with my eyes aimed always ahead I expected to be occupied mostly with memories or reveries.

I intended to spend two days in the capital city and to stay with a man and his wife who had been my friends since our childhood nearly sixty years before. The man and his wife lived in an inner south-eastern suburb, in the same house that the man had lived in nearly sixty years before when I had first visited him from the outer south-eastern suburb where I then lived. The man's mother had died when he was a child, and he lived in the house with his older brother, their father, and an unmarried middle-aged woman who was their father's cousin and who kept house for him and his sons. After my friend had left home as a young adult, I did not visit the house for fifty years, and when I next visited it the house had been thoroughly altered inside, although its outward appearance had not changed, the walls being still of white-painted timber and the return veranda leading still from the front door to the side door.

For as long as I was inside the altered house, I could not remember how it had formerly looked. Whenever I was far away from the house, I was able to recall certain details of the former interior, but they seemed to belong to a house that I had not visited since I was a boy. On my first visit to the house, nearly sixty years ago, I had noticed panes of coloured glass in the front door, in the door leading inwards from the end of the return veranda, and above the bow-windows of several rooms. On my first visit to the house after an absence of fifty years, the coloured glass was the first detail that I noticed. I could not recall any of the colours and designs that I had seen long before but I had no doubt that the panes had not been replaced during renovations. Yet the sight of the glass in no way helped me to reconcile my two sets of memories. Whenever I was a guest of my friend and his wife, I was quite unable to recall the earlier house, so to call it. Whenever I was out of sight of the house, I was able again to recall the earlier house but as though it was a different house from the later. (This might have been hardly worth my reporting here except that it seems to justify a claim made by the narrator of some or another work of fiction that I last looked into perhaps thirty years ago and the title of which I have forgotten: what we call *time* is no more than our awareness of place after place as we move continuously through endless space.) As for the coloured glass, I saw the same colours and shapes in each mental image but in different surroundings. Moreover, each of the two images of coloured panes affected me differently.

Whenever I remembered the house of fifty or more years before, the coloured leaf-shapes and petal-shapes and stem-shapes and the other shapes that signified nothing to me—those shapes seemed connected with the olden days, as I would have called the few decades leading back from the year of my birth to the beginning of the twentieth century. The woman who kept house for the motherless boys and their widower-father, she who was always called *Aunt* by my friend, had grey hair and peered through spectacles with thick lenses. She said little to my friend and nothing to me for as long as I was in the house. My friend had told me that she went to her room every evening as soon as she had washed and dried the dishes. She would never listen to the radio. It was understood that she spent much of her time in her room reading from the Bible. Every Sunday she went to some or another Protestant church. That was all that I knew about the woman. When I thought of the olden days, I had in my mind an image of a younger version of the grey-haired woman as she taught a Sunday-school class or while she sat at a piano and played hymn-tunes to her parents and siblings of a Sunday evening or while she dusted every day the photographs on the piano and on the nearby mantelpiece, one of which may have been a photograph of a young man in military uniform, a friend of the family who had written to her once from his troopship and once from Egypt and who might have courted her, so she often supposed, if only he had returned from the Great War. Whenever I had caught sight of the panes of coloured glass during my visits long ago, I had felt a mild gloom. The pale-coloured flower-shapes might have been derived from the far-away garden that appeared in the mind of a solitary grey-haired woman whenever she prayed her dreary Protestant prayers, hoping to meet up in paradise with her lost young suitor.

During my visits to the restored house, so to call it, I looked boldly and often at the coloured glass. I understood that every detail there was exactly as it had appeared to me fifty years before, and yet I got from my sight of those details a certain reassurance and satisfaction. My friend and his wife and I had outlived by far the persons who had once had power over us. We no longer had to defer to parents or to fear the disapproval of church-going aunts. Customs that had bound us in former times we now joked about at dinner-tables in newly restored houses where the so-called features were often the same furnishings or fittings that had bored us or intimidated us long before. The same coloured glass that I had once thought suitable for the middle-aged or the unmarried now reminded me of the good taste of my friends and contemporaries who were saving from decay the houses of the inner suburbs and preserving their quainter details.

I had never been able to read or hear the words *spirit* or *soul* or *psyche* without my seeing a mental image of an ovoid or diamond-shaped or rhomboidal or many-sided zone of one or more colours superimposed on or congruent with or permeating the space occupied by the inner organs of its possessor. I have asked myself often what are the origins of this image. I have sometimes supposed that I was influenced as a child by the rainbow-flashes I saw when sunlight fell at a certain angle on the bevelled edge of a mirror hanging in the lounge-room of a cream-coloured house mentioned elsewhere in this report, in which room everything seemed to me tasteful and elegant. Whatever are the origins of the image, its details owe much to my having heard fifty years ago from a young acquaintance of mine that his first notable experience after he had taken the hallucinogenic drug that he regularly took was his having a skull not of bone but of translucent glass through which his thoughts appeared as teeming points of one or another primary colour. During one of my first visits to my friend and his wife in their newly renovated house, and while the afternoon sunlight reached us through the coloured borders of the lounge-room window, it seemed to me suddenly self-evident that each of us three was defined not merely by a wrinkled face and body but by some or another intricate design or structure by definition invisible, even if it appeared to me as a fantastic counterpart of the glowing glass at the edge of my view just then. On the first evening of my latest visit to the capital city, after I had lain down to sleep in one of the front rooms of my friend and his wife's house, and while I studied the appearance of the three panes above the bow-window above my bed, which panes were partly lit by a streetlight, I thought of adopting for the remainder of my life the beliefs of an animist so that I could not only think of every person and every living being as possessing an inner luminous essence but could speculate often as to the colours of one after another of those glass-like entities against one after another source of light.

So thoroughly had the house been renovated, and so few were my memories from my visits there long before, that I did not know who had formerly occupied the bedroom where I lay. Perhaps my friend had slept there as a boy and a young man, he who told me often during our schooldays that he had watched on the previous evening this or that film in this or that cinema in this or that suburb adjoining his own and had afterwards seen in his dark bedroom this or that image of this or that female film-star. My friend's father indulged the motherless boy, who was free to go to the cinema whenever he chose. I lived at that time in an outer suburb towards the end of a railway line that passed through my friend's suburb. Even if cinemas had been near by, and even if my parents could have found the money, I would not have been permitted to watch more than an occasional film. Sometimes an image of a female film-star would appear to me in my darkened bedroom, but the image was usually of black and white and grey, being derived from some or another newspaper illustration. Most of the images of females that appeared to me were derived from persons that I had seen while I travelled by train to and from the inner eastern suburb where I attended secondary school, and even though I had first seen those persons in daylight, their images seemed to me less lively and less vivid than if they had been derived from close-up views of film-stars such as my friend sometimes described to me.

Whatever sort of image-female appeared to me after dark, I understood that my image-dalliance with her was an offence against Almighty God: a grave sin that I would later have to confess to a priest. Things were far otherwise with my friend. His mother had been a churchgoer, and his father, who claimed to have no religious beliefs, had sent the boy to church each Sunday as his mother would have wished. However, according to my friend, he took no part in the service but sat idly in a rear seat. He had never, so he said, given the least credence to anything taught him by nuns, brothers, or priests. What I thought of as the vast depository of the Faith was for him on a level with fairy stories. I envied him his composure whenever he dismissed in a few words something that I felt obliged to comprehend; to translate into clear visual imagery. When I asked him as a boy of fourteen what the word *God* brought to his mind, he claimed to see an image of a church with its windows empty and only its walls standing, like an illustration he had once seen of the ruins of Tintern Abbey in England.

Lying as an elderly man in the room where my friend might have lain nearly sixty years before, I was no more able than I had been as a boy to envisage whatever nothingness or absence might have appeared to my friend whenever he heard such terms as *heaven* or *after-life*. I stared at the coloured panes above the window-blind and thought of technicolour imagery on screens in darkened suburban cinemas long since demolished.

Sometimes before I slept, I supposed that I was in the room that had been the bedroom of my friend's wifeless father or of the single lady his cousin. The father, when I knew him, had seemed an old man although he was nearly twenty years younger than I am as I write this paragraph. He was a man of many prejudices who often irritated me. He had never attended any church except for the occasion of his wedding, and yet he often urged his son and me to be true to our religion. He had drunk much beer in his early years, but I knew him as a teetotaller who preached against strong drink. He died in his eightieth year, and his funeral service was conducted by the minister from his cousin's church, who had obviously never met the man. Whenever I thought I was lying in his former room, I supposed he might sometimes have consoled himself during his thirty and more years as a widower with imagery derived from the few Sunday-school sessions that he might have attended as a boy. Lying beneath faintly lit seeming-representations of stems and leaves and petals, I thought of a man who thought of the virtuous as strolling after death in an endless garden or park. I had learned from my friend that his father had lived as a boy in many districts and knew little about his forebears but that he often spoke as though he was somehow connected with a certain township in the central highlands of the state. This township was no great distance to the east from the huge expanse of mostly treeless grazing land that I drove across on my journey from just short of the border to the capital city. For much of my life, I supposed that I could travel only westward if ever I should move from the capital city. Even when I seemed to have decided to spend all my life in that city, I stipulated in my last Will that my remains should be buried in the west of the state. It was easy for me to assume that the father of my friend, when he heard as a boy from the young woman his Sunday-school teacher that heaven was a beautiful garden or that heaven had many mansions—that the boy would think of what lay to the west of him; would think of the mostly level and treeless district where I sometimes noticed a certain word on a signpost and then began to think of a mansion with a return veranda overlooking paddocks where racehorses were bred. Many years later, so I supposed many years later still, the middle-aged widower who was formerly the boy just mentioned called to mind before he fell asleep an image of his dead wife strolling in an image-garden surrounding an image-mansion with a return veranda in the district that still seemed always to the west of him.

Sometimes I supposed that the room where I was lying had been, fifty years before, the room where my friend's so-called aunt had read her Bible every evening while her widower-cousin listened to the radio or watched television and while his motherless son was at the cinema. I supposed the middle-aged woman had often had in mind an image of the young male personage that she would have called her saviour or her redeemer or her lord. I was unable to conceive of the woman's mental image as differing in any way from the image of the same male personage who had appeared often to me as a boy and a young man. Even fifty years after I had decided that the image was no more than an image, I could easily call to mind the youngish image-man with chestnut-coloured hair falling to his shoulders and wearing a long cream-coloured robe beneath a crimson cloak. One source of this image may have been the illustration on the certificate that had been presented to me on the occasion of my first communion. In the illustration, an image of the youngish man with the chestnut-coloured hair is holding in front of the face of a kneeling image-boy a tiny glowing image-object that he would have lifted out, moments before, from a golden chalice-shaped image-vessel. A shaft of image-light falls diagonally across the scene from somewhere outside the dark margins of the illustration. The colour of these rays allows me to suppose that one or more windows lie outside the margins mentioned and that one at least of the windows contains an area of glass of a colour between gold and red.

After I had written the previous paragraph, I took the certificate mentioned out from the folder where it has lain out of sight for perhaps twenty years in one of my filing cabinets. I was not surprised to find in the illustration a number of details differing from those in the image that I had in mind while I wrote the previous paragraph. Even the image-boy and the young image-man with the chestnut-coloured hair were posed differently and with different facial expressions from their counterparts in my remembered version of the illustration. The one detail that seemed identical in both the actual and the remembered illustration was the light falling diagonally from an unseen source. In the course of many years, I had allowed myself to falsify, as it were, the central images of the illustration:

the image-boy receiving the gift of the Blessed Sacrament from his image-saviour. And yet I seemed to have been at pains to keep in mind the precise appearance of a certain shaft of light, which was the only evidence for the existence of a certain invisible window of invisible colours somewhere in the invisible world whence arises the subject-matter of illustrations.

If I suppose myself to be occupying the room formerly occupied by the so-called aunt, then I sometimes suppose that she was sometimes visited before sleep by an image of the young man who wrote a letter to her while he was travelling by ship across the Indian Ocean and a further letter while he was camped in Egypt and who might have written more letters to her and might later have proposed marriage to her if only he had not been killed in action soon after he had been sent ashore on the Gallipoli Peninsula. Some of the images, so I supposed, would have been of the young man in a soldier's uniform, but these interested me less than the images of the young man after he had returned home safe and well, and after he had married the young woman, the recipient of the letters mentioned and of many subsequent letters. (As a student of mental imagery, I am interested to note that the images mentioned in the previous sentence appeared to me as clearly as any other images mentioned in this report or any other images that have appeared to me; and yet they were images of images that might have appeared at least thirty years before to a middle-aged or elderly woman who is no longer alive; moreover, the images that might have appeared to the woman were of a young man as he might have appeared if he had not already died.)

The images mentioned did not lack clarity, but I admit that a few details were blurred. I have never taken any interest in the clothing of earlier periods, much less in military uniforms or service medals or such things. I believe that my images of the young man in uniform derive from my having seen nearly forty years ago in a biography of the English poet Edward Thomas a reproduction of a photograph of the poet in uniform soon after he had enlisted for service in the First World War, in the course of which he was killed in action. My interest in Edward Thomas arose not from an interest in his poems, hardly any of which I have read, but from my having once read his biography of the English prose writer Richard Jefferies.

When I visualise the house where the imagined husband and wife first lived after their marriage, the front elevation derives from no house that I recall having seen. My view of the kitchen, however, includes several images that derive from details of the kitchen in the weatherboard house where I lived for several years as a boy in the provincial city mentioned earlier in this report. The detail that most deserves mention is the sink, so to call it. When I lived in the house mentioned, more than sixty years ago, the word *sink* referred only to the basin of chipped and stained porcelain beneath the tap. The place to one side of the sink where utensils were stood or food was prepared was called the *draining-board* and was of wood. When the draining-board had first been fitted, it would have contained perhaps six deep grooves. These grooves, like the surface of the whole draining-board, sloped slightly towards the sink. By the time when my family had moved into the weatherboard house, the surface of the draining-board had been so worn as to be almost smooth. Even so, the scrubbed and bleached wood was still sufficiently indented for me to be able to use it as the site for pretend-footraces.

In many a town or city to the north of the capital city of this state was run during my youth a footrace with a considerable cash prize for the winner. Each race was decided by the running of first heats and then semi-finals and, towards the end of the day, the final. None of these events was contested by more than six runners, each of whom followed his own path from the starting blocks to the finishing tape, which path was marked out by a length of string on either side, the string being kept by metal pegs at the height of a man's knee. Each of the six men in each race wore a singlet of a colour that distinguished him from his fellows. The man who was handicapped to start at the rear wore red; the man second from the rear wore white; the others wore, in order, blue, yellow, green, and pink, if I remember rightly. Sometimes, on a quiet afternoon, when my mother had cleaned the kitchen after lunch and had not yet begun to prepare the evening meal, I stood for perhaps an hour at the sink while I decided the outcome of a pretend-race with a rich prize. The contestants were as many of my glass marbles as had for their predominant colour one or another of the colours mentioned above. I decided each heat or semi-final or final by having six marbles roll across the draining-board, one in each groove, before falling into the sink, where a folded tea-towel protected the marbles from being damaged by the porcelain.

Given that the so-called aunt was the cousin of the widower who was my friend's father, I have always supposed that she would have looked forward to settling after her marriage in a township that she was somehow connected with. In short, I saw a cottage that surely had a wooden draining-board in its kitchen. I saw that cottage as standing in a township mentioned previously on the margins of the plateau mentioned several times previously in this report. The cottage would have been a humble rented cottage, and the returned soldier would have been an unskilled farm-labourer. I had heard from my friend that his father had often tramped the countryside as a young man looking for work during the so-called Great Depression and had been grateful to the proprietor of a troupe of boxers who travelled through the inland parts of several states and set up his tent at one after another annual show. The proprietor had employed the young man to stand on a platform outside the tent and to persuade young men from the crowd to challenge the members of the troupe to box for an agreed sum of money. The young man was paid no wages for his work, but the owner of the troupe bought him a meal in a café each evening and a pot of beer in a hotel.

If her cousin had once worked for no more than a meal and a pot of beer, how grateful would the young wife have been, and how sincerely would she have thanked God in her prayers every night, after her husband had found employment on the largest property in the district: a wide expanse of mostly level grazing land on the plateau mentioned previously, with plantations of black-green cypress trees forming stripes and bars on the otherwise bare paddocks, emerald green for half the year and yellow-brown for the other half. It was not God who arranged this, of course, but I, a man she knew nothing of.

She had taken no notice of me during my few visits to her widower-cousin's house fifty years before, nor did I know even the year of her death. I had decided, however, while I was falling asleep in the room where she herself might often have fallen asleep that the best of the possible lives that she might have imagined herself as living was as the wife of an employee on the large property mentioned, where not only sheep and cattle grazed but thoroughbred horses also.

At first the young husband rode his bicycle between the property where he worked and the township where he lived. Later, he moved with his wife and their first child into one of the cottages provided for workers on the large property. That was as far as I followed the story, so to call it, of the persons seen in her mind by the young woman whose image was sometimes in my mind while I lay before sleep in the room where the so-called aunt may once have lain while the upper panes of the window beside me were mildly coloured by the light from a streetlamp outside. I left the story thus suspended because I supposed that the so-called aunt was unable to conceive of any more desirable way of life than to live on a large grazing property in a cottage provided by the owner of the property. My having supposed this implies that I myself, in a certain mood or under certain conditions, am likewise unable.

I have not yet forgotten the period of my life when I read book after book of fiction in the belief that I would learn thereby matters of much importance not to be learned from any other kind of book. I have not yet forgotten the appearance of the rooms where my books (most of them works of fiction) stood on shelf after shelf. I have not yet forgotten the places where I sat reading. I am able to recall many of the dust-jackets or the paper covers of the books that I read and even particular mornings or afternoons or evenings when I read. I certainly recall some of what took place in my mind while I read; I can recall many images that occurred to me and many moods that overcame me, but the words and sentences that were in front of my eyes when the images occurred or the moods arose—of those countless items I recall hardly any.

What is the name of the author of a certain collection of pieces of short fiction that I read perhaps thirty years ago? I remember nothing of my experience as a reader of his fiction, but I remember the import of a few sentences in an introductory essay at the head of the fiction. The works of fiction had been translated from the German language, and the author of the essay seemed to have assumed that the author of the fiction would have been previously unknown to English-speaking readers. At the time when I read the essay and the fiction, I was a husband and the father of several young children. The small house where I lived was so crowded that I had to keep my books in the lounge-room and in the central passage. The books were shelved in alphabetical order according to the surnames of their authors. The collection with the introductory essay was kept on one of the lowest shelves in the passage. The surname of the author must therefore have begun with one of the last letters of the English alphabet. Whoever he was, I have remembered about him for perhaps thirty years that he could conceive of no more fulfilling way of life than that of a servant: a person scarcely ever required to instigate or to decide matters but able instead to experience the peculiar joy that comes from carrying out an instruction to the letter or from following the strictest of daily routines. I have just now seemed to remember about the author that he spent much of his later life, and may well have died, in a lunatic asylum, so to call it, but this has not dissuaded me from stating here that I am much in sympathy with the man as I seem to remember him. Nor am I dissuaded from thinking of the young woman and the husband mentioned as being content to spend the remainder of their lives as the writer in the German language claimed to want to spend his life with the difference, perhaps, that the writer might have wanted to spend the last hour of every evening in his tiny room with pen and paper, writing one after another work of fiction of the sort that I once read but later forgot whereas the young woman and her husband might have wanted no more, before they fell asleep, than to see in mind some little of what they had failed to see by day: she, perhaps, the huge, dim rooms on the far side of some or another window when the afternoon sunlight picked out the fields of colours in its panes; he, perhaps, the faces of the young female persons whose voices he sometimes heard from behind the vine-covered trellises on the long return veranda at the far side of the wide lawns and the symmetrically located flower-beds and fishponds.

(Whenever I recall, here in this quiet district near the border, my mostly aimless activity during my fifty and more years in the capital city, I begin to envy the sort of man who might have been paid a modest wage during most of his adult life in return for feeding and watering and grooming and exercising a half-dozen thoroughbred horses in a certain few sheds and paddocks behind a plantation of cypresses on the far side of an assortment of outbuildings in the vicinity of an immense garden surrounding a sprawling homestead out of sight of the nearest road, which would have appeared as one of the faintly coloured least of roads if ever I had seen it on some or another map of some or another of the mostly level grassy landscapes that seem often to lie in some or another far western district of my mind.)

I reported in the fourth most recent paragraph that I was accustomed to leaving the sequence of imaginings of the so-called aunt suspended at a certain point. While I was writing the two previous paragraphs, however, a number of image-events occurred to me such as might readily have prolonged the sequence while keeping it still relevant to this report. The first of the possible events is the so-called aunt's giving birth to a daughter at about the time when my own birth took place. (Several problems kept me at first from moving beyond this event. According to the time-scale that I had in mind, this birth would have taken place nearly twenty years after the so-called aunt's marriage and when she was nearly forty years of age. At that period of history, such a birth would have been by no means improbable, but it was likely to have been the ninth or tenth of its kind, so that the daughter would have been the youngest of numerous siblings. This was not to my liking. I wanted better for the daughter than that she would have been the ninth or tenth child of a farm-labourer; that she should wear hand-me-down clothes and lack for finery and toys and have to do housework when she might otherwise have been reading or day-dreaming. I was ready to decree that the child should have been adopted by the so-called aunt after she had been childless for many years—a pampered only child better suited my narrative than a threadbare child-drudge—until I recalled the girl-woman who had once guided me towards a fishpond overhung by leaves of a certain shade of red. She had been the only child of a mother whose hair was greying. A quite separate problem was that I seemed to be calling into existence the daughter and her circumstances as though I and not the so-called aunt was lying before sleep in a room with coloured panes in its window and envisaging possible events. But this ceased to seem a problem after I had reminded myself that this is a report of actual events and no sort of work of fiction. As I understand the matter, a writer of fiction reports events that he or she considers imaginary. The reader of the fiction considers, or pretends to consider, the events actual. This piece of writing is a report of actual events only, even though many of the reported events may seem to an undiscerning reader fictional.)

The daughter, as I intend to call her, had an upbringing rather different from mine. I lived at times in suburbs of the capital city and at other times in a provincial city or in a remote district of mostly treeless countryside where three previous generations of my father's family had lived but where I never felt at home because the district was bounded on one side by ocean. She lived until she was almost a young woman in the one house on a far-reaching plateau, seeing every day views of mostly level grassy countryside such as I knew for many years only from illustrations. One of the houses that I lived in had in one door a pane of coloured glass. She saw every day not only the coloured panes in several doors of her own house but distant views of many a door and many a window of a mansion in room after room of which, on walls or floors or furnishings, were zones of subdued colour where fell in early morning or late afternoon what sunlight was still able to reach beneath the beetling iron roof and through the vines and creepers of the return veranda. Her parents may not have been regular churchgoers but they had been married before a clergyman and they sent their daughter to the Sunday school conducted by the same Protestant denomination that built a certain church of pale-coloured stone and fitted in the porch of the church a coloured window the sight of which prompted me to begin writing this report. Her upbringing and mine were rather different, but she and I, like almost every other young person of our time and place, had been compelled during year after year of our childhood, during freezing mornings or hot afternoons, to find interest, or to pretend to find interest in one or another of a series of reading books compiled by the Department of Education in our state and sold cheaply to all schools, whether state or denominational. Capable readers such as she and I read the whole of our reader, as it was called, during the first few days after we had taken possession of it. Then, during the remainder of the year, we were obliged to sit during so-called reading lessons while one or another of our classmates read aloud laboriously some or another paragraph from some or another prose item that we, the capable readers, had long ago tired of reading. The reading books were first published ten years before my birth and were in widespread use for nearly thirty years afterwards. During those years, many schools, whether state or denominational, were so poorly equipped that pupils read no other books than their readers. This was certainly so in the schools that I attended, and I could not have begun to write this paragraph if it had not been so in the school that the daughter attended.

The daughter and I were sometimes repelled, not so much by the subject-matter of many items in the readers as by their moral overtones. Neither she nor I could have devised such an expression—we might have said that the compilers of the readers, if not the authors of the texts themselves, were preaching at us. Sometimes their preaching was strident, but even when they preached subtly we were alert to them, we who had been preached at so often as children by parents and teachers and pastors. The readers contained many illustrations, but all were black and white. The daughter and I understood that coloured illustrations would have made the readers prohibitively expensive, but we wondered why so many of the line-drawings failed to attract us and so many of the reproductions of photographs were murky and their details blurred, and we even fancied sometimes that the stylised children in the line-drawings and the grey landscapes in the half-tone reproductions had a moral purpose: to remind us that life was a serious matter. Very few items in the readers were overtly religious. I recall only an extract from *The Pilgrim's Progress*, an account of the Pilgrim Fathers' first years in America, and my learning from the notes at the rear of one of the readers that John Milton, the author of several extracts in the series, was the Poet of Puritan England and second only to Shakespeare. Even so, I often felt as though every one of the readers had been put together single-handedly by a well-intentioned but tiresome

Protestant clergyman. As a boy, I could not have distinguished between the various Protestant denominations, but thirty-five years later I talked at length with a woman whose thesis for a higher degree in education had argued that the implicit message of the series of readers embodied, as she put it, the world-view of Nonconformism in the early decades of the twentieth century.

And yet the readers contained items that the daughter and I were apt to remember throughout our lives. For whatever reason, the compilers of the series had included in each volume one or two items that were not only free from preachiness but likely to leave a child-reader at least pensive, if not troubled. In one of the many possible lives that I might have led, the daughter and I met as young persons and began to keep company. Among the many things that we were pleased to talk about were the freezing mornings or hot afternoons when each of us searched the school reader for one of the few pieces able to lead our thoughts away from the unhospitable classroom, the moralising text read haltingly aloud by one after another of our dull classmates, the cheerless illustrations. I was pleased to hear from her that she read often and pondered over the story of the mare employed during her last years as a pit-pony who was fond of telling the foal born to her underground about the green meadows and the blue skies she had once seen, even though the foal thought the mare's tales were imaginings and the mare herself began at last to be of the same opinion. She, the daughter, was pleased to hear from me that I had likewise read and pondered over the poem about the old horse that had been harnessed for most of its life to a capstan-like device at a mine and compelled to trudge continually in circles until a time when the mine was abandoned and the horse was put to pasture near by but loitered until the last hour of its life as near as it could draw to the place where it had formerly toiled and suffered. I was pleased to hear that she had read often and pondered over the poem about the toys that had been gathering dust and turning to rust for year after year but were still waiting faithfully for the return of their owner, the small boy who had set them in place but had still not returned. She was pleased to hear that I had likewise read and pondered over the poem reporting the thoughts and imaginings of the poet while he stood at evening in a country graveyard and pondered on the possible lives that might have been lived by the persons whose remains were buried near by.

While I was writing the previous three paragraphs, I had at hand a complete set of the readers mentioned: facsimiles of the original books issued as a commemorative edition twenty-five years ago. After I had finished writing the previous paragraph, I turned to the pages where was printed the third of the poems mentioned in that paragraph. I was surprised to find that the text published in the reader was an abridged text. Missing from the text that I read often as a boy were several stanzas of the original, most notably the last stanza, in which the Deity is mentioned reverently. I can hardly believe that the poem was abridged because space was short in the pages of the reader. Nor can I readily believe that the compilers of the series of readers would have censored, as it were, what they would have considered a masterpiece of English literature. I can only marvel at the seemingly inexplicable circumstance that the possible self of mine who sometimes seemed to stand beside the personage seemingly responsible for the writing of a certain famous English poem—that one of my possible selves was never obliged at last to bow his head and to lower his eyes and to feign devotedness to the divine personage in whose honour had been built the church near by but was instead free to look up from among the graves and the headstones and to observe from a distance the subdued glow effected by the setting sun in at least one coloured pane of one window.

The daughter had an upbringing rather different from mine but each of us sometimes, during one or another of my possible lives, recounted something that surprised the other and made his or her secret history seem explicable after all. I would have been thus surprised when she first told me that she had sometimes during her childhood arranged on the mat in her lounge-room glass beads from her mother's sewing basket. The beads were of different colours, and she arranged them as the images of coloured jackets of jockeys were arranged on the far side of an image-racecourse in her mind whenever she heard on some or another afternoon certain indistinct sounds from which she understood that her father's employer, the owner of the far-reaching property where she lived, was listening on the return veranda of his mansion to a radio broadcast of some or another race contested by one or another of his horses on some or another distant racecourse.

When I last travelled to the capital city, I took with me a camera with a roll of unexposed film inside. On the last morning of my stay in the weatherboard house mentioned earlier, I prepared to photograph each of the coloured panes in each of the windows and doors overlooking the driveway and the return veranda.

Whenever I return from the capital city to this border district, I set out in the early morning. After I had eaten my breakfast and stored my luggage in my car on the last morning mentioned above, the sun had still not risen, although the few clouds in the pale sky were already pink. My friend and his wife were still in their own wing of the house, almost certainly still asleep. I stepped quietly along the veranda and the driveway, taking one shot of each pane from the outside. Then I crept through the lounge-room, my own room, the passage, and my friend's study, taking one shot of each pane from the inside. In the last city along my homeward route, I left the film to be developed and printed. I have since collected two postcard-sized prints of each exposure. The prints are beside me as I write. During the days before I collected the prints, I hoped to learn from them something of value. I looked forward to inspecting the prints at my leisure. Not since my childhood had I felt free to look through coloured panes for as long as I might have wanted to look. In all my adult life, I had merely glanced or looked sideways at such things, partly from my belief, mentioned earlier, that a glance or a sideways look often reveals more than a direct gaze and partly from my reluctance to make any sort of show of my interests or motives. (My writing this report is no violation of my long-standing policy. These pages are intended only for my files.) In fact, my first inspection of the prints, after I had fetched them safely to my room yesterday, consisted of my first scattering them on the bare surface of this desk and then looking towards them from various points while I paced about the room. I tried to look at the prints as though unaware of what they might have depicted. Some of what I saw brought to mind drooping leaves, wing-cases of beetles, crucifixes bare of human figures but oozing coloured droplets, feathers fallen from birds in flight . . . Later, after I had sat at the desk and had looked more closely, I was reminded of what I had surely learned long before, although I had seemed to note it for the first time while I was puzzling recently over the window in my neighbourhood church: that a coloured pane better reveals itself to a viewer on its darker side, so to call it; that the colours and designs in glass windows are truly apparent only to an observer shut off from what most of us would consider true light—the light best able to do away with mystery and uncertainty. This paradox, if such it is, can be otherwise expressed: anyone observing the true appearance of a coloured window is unable, for the time being, to observe through that window any more than a falsification of the so-called everyday world. I was reminded of this when I compared each pair of photographs of one and the same window: one photograph taken from outside in the early morning light and the other photograph taken from inside the dim house. These matters hardly surprised me, but I remain still puzzled by a second discovery. In the first minutes while I inspected the prints, I found myself several times about to lift one or the other print and to hold it between my face and the desk-lamp. At first, I supposed I was prompted by a sort of instinctive curiosity; I had in my hands accurate evidence of sights I had been eager to record, but then, quite unthinkingly, I made as though to learn more than was in my power to learn. And so, I caught myself several times preparing to look through, or more deeply into, what was hardly more than dyed paper. After I had several times almost given way to this child-like impulse, another explanation occurred to me. I had photographed my friends' windows and doors hardly more than a week before. I could recall clearly not just my stepping along the return veranda and the driveway and in through the two doors leading from the return veranda into the house; I could recall clearly the colour of the sky and of the few clouds at the time; and I could certainly recall the sight of each area of coloured glass when I aimed my camera at it—not the sight of each of the many details in each pane but the degree of clarity and the intensity of the colour in the most noticeable of those details. I recalled these things, and at the same time I was aware that the image-panes on the desk before me seemed less colourful than the actual panes when I had photographed them. I might have decided that this discrepancy was caused by my lack of skill as a photographer, even though the camera had been switched to *automatic* at the time. Ignorant as I am in the fields of optics and physics, I might have decided that no photographic film is quite so sensitive to light as is the human retina. I might simply have decided that I imagined rather than recalled the sight of the actual windows: that this was one more example of the unreliability of memory. Instead, I chose to subscribe for the time being to a quaint-seeming theory of vision mentioned earlier in this report. I even modified or expanded this theory, or what little I had once read about it, when I decided that my seeing the panes of glass in the early morning had consisted of much more than my registering, as it were, certain shapes and colours; that a part of my seeing was my investing the glass with qualities not inherent in it—qualities probably not apparent to any other observer and certainly not detectable by any sort of camera; that what I missed when I looked at the photographic prints was the meaning that I had previously read into the glass. And if I could give credence to such an eccentric theory, then I might as well go further and assert that I saw in the glass part of the private spectrum that my eyes diffused from my own light as it travelled outwards: a refraction of my own essence, perhaps.

This township is about half-way between the city where I formerly lived, which is the capital city of this state, and the capital city of the adjoining state, where I have still not yet been. I get my news from newspapers. I own no television set or computer, but I brought with me to this house a twenty-five-years-old radio that can be used to play audio cassettes. On several evenings each week, I listen to some or other of the fifty and more tapes, as I call them, that I recorded during the fourth and fifth decades of my life, when I still believed in the power of music to cause me to see what I had never seen with my eyes. The pieces of taped music, so to call it, were only some of many pieces of music that brought to my mind, whenever I heard them, unfolding images of mostly level grassy landscapes. As a young man, I chose to consider the landscapes an actual part of my mind that I might never have discovered had I not heard the pieces of music. (For most of my life, I have only pretended to acknowledge the claims of so-called common sense. I could never accept, for example, that my mind

97

is a creation, much less a function, of my brain.) While I considered them thus, I enjoyed the landscapes as spectacles, which is to say that I seemed to view the landscapes as though they comprised a topographical map over which I passed as a low-flying bird might pass. Sometimes, I enjoyed as well the conviction that the seeming progression of the landscape across the range of my vision, or my seeming myself to be progressing across the landscapes, was a sort of a prefiguration of a future journey that I had first seemed likely to make on certain mornings during my schooldays when I translated into English one after another page of the book-length Latin poem recounting the journey of certain fugitives from Troy towards their destined homeland. (Few persons of my place and time can have travelled less often and less far than I. The only journey of mine that might seem the fulfilment of my youthful daydreams is the journey that I made last year to this township, unless the unthinkable happens and I find some agreeable last haven on the other side of the border.)

I experienced as a reader of fiction much of what I experienced as a listener to music, but with the important difference that the fictional texts that I read contained many an explicit description of some or another landscape. Reading sentence after sentence containing detail after detail of some or another such landscape, I was able to value the resulting mental imagery for its uniqueness; to see it lying in the marches between the mental territories of reader and writer. I still look sometimes into works of fiction but I read few of them to the end. Among the most recent works that I succeeded in reading is an English translation of a novel of three volumes first published in the Hungarian language in the decade before my birth and set, so to speak, in the region called in English Transylvania but in Hungarian Erdély. Until 1919, Transylvania had been not only part of the Kingdom of Hungary but the site of the purest form of Hungarian culture, the one region that had never been invaded during the two centuries when the Turks had ruled most of Hungary. The author had written his work of three volumes during the decade after 1919, in which year Transylvania had become part of Romania under the terms of the Treaty of Trianon, but the action of the novel took place, so to speak, in previous decades. The narrator of the novel was far from regarding the pre-war period as a Golden Age; he recognised the follies of the Hungarian rulers of what was soon to become their lost province. Only when he wrote about the landscapes of Transylvania did he seem to give way to regret. Many a chapter of his novel began with a page and more of lavish description of some or another river-valley between forested foothills of the Transylvanian Alps. So heartfelt were some of these descriptions that I had sometimes to remind myself that the scenery I was reading about was no long-lost country of dreams but had still been in place when the book had been written; had not been abolished by any treaty between nations; was still in existence even while I was reading. The same rivers flowed between the same forested hillsides with the same snowy peaks in the background, and yet the narrator described the scenery as though it was soon to pass from sight forever. And so it was, if I think of the sight of a landscape as inseparable from the person having sight of it. If I think thus, then what were reported in the lavish descriptions, as I called them, were no mere landscapes but semblances of river-valleys and forests and folds of mountains illuminated by the regard of a man with translucent panes for eyes.

This matter of the landscapes was not what first prompted me to write about the novel of three volumes. I intended to report a simple discovery that I made when I was reading an especially detailed description of a landscape in the fictional Transylvania where the novel is set. At one point when I was reading a long report of meadows, of fast-flowing streams, of forests, of mountains, and even of clouds and sky, I paused to observe what was taking place in my mind. I found that I was far from assembling there a detailed landscape, adding or adjusting this or that item as my eyes passed over this or that word or phrase or sentence. What seemed to have happened was that a certain image-landscape had appeared to me as soon as I had begun to read the long report and had learned from the first sentence or from my glancing at the text ahead what was the subject of the report. This image-landscape remained almost unchanged in my mind while I read the entire report. If I happened to read a reference to the rooftops of a distant village, then there appeared in my original landscape a few vague patches meant to suggest thatched roofs, and if I learned from my reading that a horse-drawn carriage was to be seen on a road near the village, then a simple image appeared of a toy-like coach on a stylised road. Otherwise, my original image, so to call it, persisted unaltered. In spite of all that I read, no far-reaching water-meadows, no beetling cliffs, and no hurtling streams found their way into my simple mental scenery, which, when I came to look at it closely, comprised a road in the foreground, a few green paddocks in the middle ground, and the abrupt slope of a forested mountain in the background. I knew, as I sometimes know things in dreams, that a fast-flowing creek or river lay out of sight where the last paddock ended and the forested slope began. Sometimes, the blurred details of a house with white walls and a red-brown roof appeared near the site of the unseen stream, although these details were sometimes replaced by details more in keeping with the text of the fiction.

I soon discovered the approximate source of the incongruous mental scenery. Late in my eighteenth year, I acquired my first girlfriend. I had been attracted to her by nothing more than the appearance of her face, which seemed to tell me that she was a gentle, thoughtful person who would rather listen than chatter. Perhaps she was, in fact, such a person. Certainly she was obliged to behave as such a person whenever she and I were together during the short time while we were girlfriend and boyfriend. While we travelled several times to and from a Saturday football-match in an inner suburb of the capital city, while we were together at several Sunday evening dances in the church-hall in the outer south-eastern suburb where we both lived, and while I several times took afternoon tea with the girl and her younger sister and their mother in their lounge-room, I missed no opportunity to tell her what I had been waiting for many years to tell to a sympathetic listener.

I forget almost all of the thousands of words that I spoke to the person who had seemed to me more a listener than a chatterer, but I recall some of what I felt while I spoke the words. Perhaps I should have written just then that I seem to recall not certain feelings but, rather, the fact of my having once felt these feelings. And while I was struggling to write the previous sentence, I recalled yet again the occasion that prompted me to begin writing this report: the occasion when I passed for the first time the window in the porch of my neighbourhood church and failed to identify from my vantage-point in the sunshine the colours and shapes that would have been apparent to someone in the shaded porch on the other side of the glass.

My girlfriend and I kept company, so to speak, for perhaps two months. Our last outing together was a picnic on a Sunday in early spring, in a park beside a reservoir in a range of mountains north-east of the capital city. We travelled to and from the picnic-site in a bus. All around us in the bus were other young persons from our parish, some of them in pairs like my girlfriend and myself. We two sat in a seat that took two persons only, she against the window and I nearer the aisle. I had planned during the previous week to have us seated thus; I wanted her free to look out at river-valleys or forested mountains while I went on talking to her. Apparently, I was not bereft of insight, since I remember my suspecting, late in the morning and while we were still travelling towards the picnic-site, that my girlfriend was no longer interested in what I was telling her.

Even so, I was unable to check myself and was perhaps made even more eloquent by my foreseeing that my girlfriend would tell me before the end of the day that my company was no longer agreeable to her. Much that I told her had to do with books that I had read. My talking to her allowed me to put into words what I could otherwise have expressed only in a report such as this. But I talked to her sometimes also about a book that I might one day write, and I suspect that I understood, while the bus travelled further in among the mountains, that such a book was less likely to be written by a man with an ideal female confidant than by the solitary man that I was soon to become. As for the landscape that represented for me, fifty and more years later, one after another of the lost landscapes of the author of the novel in the Hungarian language, I have no recollection of my having seen the original landscape, so to call it, anywhere among the mountains north-east of the capital city, but whenever I try to recall some or another detail from the Sunday excursion mentioned I see always in the background my own image-Transylvania.

When I turned on my old radio on the day mentioned earlier, I did so in order to listen to the broadcast of a certain horse-race. I saw from the dial that the radio was tuned, as always, to the station that broadcasts horse-races from all over the commonwealth of which this state is a part, but after I had turned on the radio the voices from the sporting station, as it was called, were continually overridden by other, louder voices. I supposed I was now so far from the capital city of my own state that my radio was receiving signals from across the border, perhaps even from the capital of the neighbouring state. I tried but could not tune the radio more closely to the sporting station. I turned up the volume. I heard, for the first time, the faint sounds of a broadcast of a horse-race but only during the brief pauses of the overriding voices, which were by now unbearably loud. They were the voices of two women, one of them apparently the presenter of a program and the other a guest being interviewed. I lowered the volume and listened, for the time being, to the two female voices.

Almost the first thing that I learned from the overriding voices was that the person being interviewed was the author of several published works of fiction. I am still willing to look into some or another work of fiction if I believe I am likely to remember afterwards even a small part of the experience; if I believe I might seem to see afterwards among the places that I call my mind some or another scenery that first appeared to me while I was reading or even a scene in which an image of myself is reading what he may later forget and, later still, may regret having forgotten. However, I have never cared to listen to persons merely talking about a book of fiction or about any sort of book as though it consists of subject-matter or ideas or topics to be talked about rather than words and sentences waiting to be read. I would have turned off my radio promptly except that the woman-author had begun to talk about a certain house of yellow- or honey-coloured stone.

The house did not exist or, rather, it existed but the author had not located it. I became strangely alert as soon as I had understood that the house might have stood at no great distance from where I sat beside my old radio in my cottage of white stone. I had earlier guessed that the author was speaking from the capital city of the adjoining state. (Her interviewer may have been questioning her from still another capital city in some further-off state, but this did not matter. For as long as the author went on talking I seemed to see her seated at a bare table in a so-called broadcasting studio, which appeared to me as a small room with tinted glass walls surrounded by many another such small room, each lit by globes obscurely placed among the many layers of tinted glass.)

The woman, as I intend to call her, had not lived for long in the neighbouring state. She had been born and had spent her childhood in a south-western county of England, and she had lived in several countries before settling in the capital city where she now lived. For the sake of her husband and her teen-aged children, she lived for the time being in an inner suburb but she spent much of her free time travelling in country districts far from the capital city. She was especially interested in what she called the far south-east of her state, which included, as I knew, the district adjoining the border on the far side of my own district. When she named some of the towns in her preferred region, I even heard the name of the place where was held the race-meeting that I had turned back from on the morning mentioned early in this report.

The woman had recently acquired a sum of money large enough for her to fulfil what she called a lifelong dream. I assumed that the money was an inheritance, although some of what was said in the interview allowed me to suppose that the woman's most recent book had won a lucrative literary prize. The lifelong dream, as she called it, was of her acquiring a certain sort of house in a certain sort of landscape and of being able to retreat to the house whenever she was in need of what she called spiritual renewal. The landscape around the house should comprise what she called long views of open country with what she called hints of forests at the margins. Her choice of such a landscape, so she explained, was the result of her childhood experiences. She had grown up in a small township near an expanse of the sort of landscape called in her native country *downs*. She had read widely from an early age and had discovered, while still a child, the works of Richard Jefferies, who had been born more than a century before her own birth and had spent his childhood on the opposite side of the downs from her own birthplace. I myself had read one of Jefferies's books during my childhood and parts of another book of his as a young man.

My father's parents had died while I was too young to be aware of them. For many years after their death, three of their daughters and one of their sons had gone on living in the family home. These four, who were, of course, aunts and an uncle of mine, were all unmarried. The house where they lived was of pale-grey stone quarried from a nearby hill. The house had a return veranda, but this had been closed off at the side of the house so as to form a sleeping-place for my uncle. In the room that my aunts called the parlour was a tall piece of furniture with its upper half comprising three shelves of books behind glass doors. During the first years when I visited the house of pale-grey stone, I was not yet capable of reading any of the books on the shelves behind the glass, or so my aunts told me. Then, on a certain afternoon while I was visiting the house during a later year, my youngest aunt took down a certain book and led me to the front veranda. We sat there together on a cane couch while she read me the first page of the book. After this, she handed me the book and asked me to read the second page. When I had read the page without stumbling, she encouraged me to go on reading and then left me alone on the veranda. I read for most of that afternoon and for most of the following two afternoons until I had finished the book, which was the longest book that I had yet read.

I remembered for long afterwards much of what I had experienced while I read the book recommended by my aunt. I still remembered some of that experience a few weeks ago, when the author from across the border first mentioned during a radio program that she had lived as a child at the opposite end of a grassy landscape from the place where the author of the book had lived as a child. However, from the moment when the author from across the border began to speak about the book as she understood it and about the author as she imagined him—from that moment, I was unable to recall any but a few persistent memories. I was no longer able, for example, to call to mind any image of the kindly if sometimes condescending middle-aged male author who had seemed sometimes to stand at the far side of my field of vision while I read. The woman his compatriot referred to him as a young man and spoke sometimes as though she might have been in love with him even though he had died nearly a century before she had been born. I still recalled that the boy who is the chief character of the book was addressed on separate occasions in English words by a swallow, a spider, a toad, and other such living things but I no longer remembered anything of what they had told him. I still remembered that the boy had sometimes been addressed by the wind, that I had sometimes had in mind while I read the purported words of the wind a translucent face against a background of leaning grass. The face had been a kindly female face, but after I had listened to the radio broadcast I could no longer call the face to mind. And yet I still recalled one item from all that the boy had heard from the wind. She had assured him that no yesterday had ever been and that no tomorrow would ever arrive.

A wind would have been blowing for much of the time while I was reading on the cane couch, but I would have taken no special note of it. The house where my aunts and uncle lived was within sight of an ocean. On the other side of the wire fence that bounded their farm to the south, the land sloped upwards towards cliff-tops above steep coves. On almost every day, a breeze or a wind blew inland across the bare paddocks. The front section of the veranda where I read was sheltered, and the sunshine was warm on my bare legs. I would have been oblivious of passing breezes, but while I was reading the reports of the speeches of the fictional wind to the fictional boy, I may well have been bothered by a continual flapping and thudding from around the corner of the return veranda. Two huge striped canvas blinds, as we called them, formed the outer walls of my uncle's sleeping-place. Each blind enclosed at its lower end a long wooden pole. At each end of each pole, a metal ring was connected by a leather strap to a similar metal ring in the wooden floor of the veranda. When the wind blew hard from the south, the canvas blinds heaved and shuddered while the metal rings rattled and tinkled. Mere noises would not have interrupted my reading, but these noises may well have reminded me that the house of pale-grey stone was not as it should have been: that the blinds and my uncle's makeshift bedroom closed off what should have been a cloister-like space for walking or for looking far outwards or even for reading in one or another of two quite different settings, one with a view inland across first a lawn of buffalo-grass and then mostly level grassy countryside and the other with a view past a low hedge of silver-grey wormwood, then a single bare paddock, and then the ocean-cliffs.

Perhaps I would also have been bothered while I read by the same incongruity that arose from much of my reading as a child: the book in front of me had been written on the far side of the world; the wind that spoke to the boy was the warm south wind that had wafted across several counties before it reached his native downlands. The wind that thumped the canvas on the southern side of the grey house was fresh from the ocean. If the return veranda had been empty and spacious as I would have preferred it, then I could have borne sometimes to feel the wind on the southern side of the house before I turned back to the calmer side overlooking the inland, but I would never have expected any sort of message to reach me from all that turbulent air.

I once read parts of an autobiographical book by Richard Jefferies. I gave up reading the book because long sections conveyed little of meaning to me. Those sections purported to describe the author's state of mind during periods of intense feeling or awareness, but they described nothing of what I call mental imagery. I learned early in my life that I am unable to comprehend the language of abstractions; for me a state of mind is incomprehensible without reference to images. The author being interviewed not only professed to admire the autobiographical book but called Richard Jefferies a profound mystic, even though he seemed to have been an atheist or, at least, to have had no belief in a personal god or even a benign creator. When she was discussing these matters the author spoke rapidly and somewhat elliptically, so that I afterward struggled to recall all that she had said, let alone to comprehend it. One thing I recall is her claim to have found much significance in the frequent references by Richard Jefferies to a certain hill near his boyhood home. His earliest mystical experiences, as she called them, had occurred to him at the age of seventeen, on one of the many mornings when he used to stand in a certain place out of doors and to watch the sun rising over the hill mentioned. Exactly a hundred years later, so the woman claimed, she herself looked on many an evening at sunset towards the same hill from the opposite direction. She may have been bending the facts a little, so she told her interviewer, but her childhood home stood in distant view of the same downs where the writer-mystic often walked or lay on certain hillsides and stared into the sky and felt the wind from the south. As for the writer's mysticism, or nature-mysticism, as she variously called it, she believed that a certain sort of insight or knowledge was incapable of being communicated from one person to another. She had read several times the author's short autobiography but she was still far from grasping what she called the inner truth of the writing. And yet this was as it should be, she said. Her own quest was not unlike that of her admired writer, but it was her own. Apart from her love of the open countryside where she had spent her childhood, the chief influence of her life had been what she called her Quaker spirituality. Her parents had been members of the Society of Friends and had taken her often as a child to their meeting-house. She was still grateful, so she said, for the tranquillity of soul that she had experienced there, and she had never ceased to believe what she had first come to believe in the silence of the meeting-house while the Friends waited to be moved by the divine presence within them. Either because she neglected to explain this belief or because I failed to grasp her explanation, I can report only that the author has faith in the existence of some or another divinity or divine principle whose presence is discernible in the human soul.

I had felt warmly towards the woman while she was talking about Richard Jefferies and his and her native landscapes, but I became wary of her after she had begun to talk about her religious beliefs. While I was still a young man, it became fashionable among some of my contemporaries to practise what they called meditation and to read books about a variety of subjects that might have been called collectively Eastern spirituality. I could never have brought myself to read any of that sort of book, but I was sometimes curious about the practice of meditation. On several mornings while my wife and children were still asleep, I sat cross-legged on a patio at the rear of my house in an outer northern suburb of the capital city. I closed my eyes and tried to breathe deeply and evenly. I then tried to perform what I believed was the next part of the process of meditation: I tried to empty my mind of the pictorial imagery and the snatches of songs or melodies that comprised its usual contents. If I could perform this task, so I supposed, then I would find myself in the presence of my mind alone, and I was curious to learn what would be the appearance of a mind devoid of contents: what my mind would prove ultimately to be composed of.

I never succeeded in emptying my mind. Several times I seemed likely to do so, but always behind my closed eyes some or another last image would disclose itself, even if it was nothing more surprising than my memory, so to call it, of the hill to the east of my house, behind which hill the sun had been about to rise when my eyes had last been open. And if, after much effort or as a result of mere chance, I had a glimpse of a seeming vacancy, of nothing but a yellowish lambency from some or another conjectured source of other than sunlight behind some or another remote inner pane, then I became again aware that the time was early morning, that the place was a suburb of my native city, and that one after another racehorse was exercising just then on each of the several racecourses in the suburbs of the same city; on racecourse after racecourse further off but still within the range of my mental vision in country district after country district in the state of which my native city was the capital; in districts where I had never been in the states adjoining my native state and in the suburbs of the capital cities of those states and of the capital cities of states further off still, not forgetting the island-state south of my own state. I forgot, or I chose to ignore, the differing time-zones of the world, and I saw horses walking or cantering or galloping on green racecourses with snow-topped mountains in the background in the country far out in the ocean southeast of my own country and on racecourse after racecourse that I knew only from illustrations in books, which racecourses were in far country after far country that I knew only from maps. I had never travelled outside my native state and seldom even outside my native city, and yet the utmost region of my mind was a vast district of image-racecourses derived mostly from images of places I had never seen.

After I had written the previous paragraph, I took out a detailed atlas of the country in which the woman and her admired Richard Jefferies had been born. A whole page was given over to the county where lay the native district of the two. Even if the woman had not mentioned during her interview certain place-names, I could have found easily enough the district I was looking for. On a page mostly crowded with networks of lines representing roads and with dots variously coloured to represent villages, townships, and every sort of larger town or city was a noticeable zone relatively unmarked. And even if I had not found on this zone the faint, widely spaced letters of the words *DOWNS* preceded by another word, I would not have failed to see the few thin, pale-blue lines representing streams that originated in the zone and led by roundabout routes away from it. Even though I had in front of my eyes only printed paper, I was able to call on some or other memories of coloured illustrations in books or magazines and so to see in mind a few stylised images of bare, domed hills and grassy uplands. I believe I intended to keep those images in mind while I tried to feel what a nature-mystic who was also an atheist might have felt in sight of the originals of such images or even what a girl or a young woman might have felt while she sat with similar images in mind in a meeting-house of the Society of Friends on a morning of bright sunshine.

Whatever were my intentions, I was unable to fulfil them after I had noticed a certain place-name at the eastern margin of the zone that had brought to my mind the stylised images mentioned above. I had seen the place-name in the captions beneath several memorable illustrations in one of my most prized volumes from what I call my horse-racing library. Some of the domed hills and grassy uplands that I had wanted to ponder on were places where numerous racehorses exercised, especially in the early morning. One of the districts adjoining the downlands had been, since the nineteenth century, the site of several famous racing stables.

I supposed that meditation and other such practices had fallen out of fashion many years ago, and if the woman-author had seemed only some latter-day believer in the mumbo-jumbo of an earlier generation I would have turned off the radio and silenced her. What kept me listening was her frequent references to the house mentioned earlier. I seemed to understand clearly enough the appearance of the house, even though the author herself had not yet seen it. What she had had for long in mind was a house of the amber-coloured sandstone that underlies a certain district in the far south-east of her state: the nearest part of her state to this far western district where I sit writing in my own state. She made no mention of such details, but I saw the house from the first as having a return veranda, panes of coloured glass at each side of the front door, and leadlight windows in the main rooms.

After the woman has found a house that meets her requirements, and after she has renovated it to her liking, she intends to make it available as a retreat for writers—but by no means

114

all writers. Anyone wanting to spend time in the retreat will first have to be interviewed by the woman and to give an account of his or her motives and aims. I remain unclear as to what sorts of writer she would most likely approve of, but I have no doubt as to her dislikes and prejudices. Playwrights and writers of film scripts she considers an inferior sub-class of writer too easily attracted by the visible and able to suggest the invisible by no other means than the gestures and grimaces of pretend-persons. She mistrusts biography, and autobiography even more so. The sort of writing that makes up this report she would surely not deign to look at, unless it could be somehow presented to her as an esoteric variety of fiction. Even in the field of fiction, she intends to exclude from the retreat all writers of romance fiction, science fiction, crime fiction, and historical fiction. If I remember rightly, several sorts of poet will not be admitted.

I understood from what I heard that the woman from across the border wants to learn how a certain sort of work of poetry or prose fiction comes into being. She hopes that some at least of the writers ensconced for the time being behind the honey-coloured stone and the coloured glass of her retreat, whether as a result of arduous self-scrutiny or following a sudden insight into his or her thoughts and feelings, will be able to explain to her what has never yet been explained, even if it may at some time have been discovered and kept secret. I gather that she will not be satisfied with any account of the creative process, so to call it, that relies on some or another fashionable theory of the mind. She claims not to understand how the term *unconscious* can be applied to any part of the mind, which she says she more readily conceives of as a luminance or glow than as any sort of organ or faculty. Given that the woman herself is an author of fiction, she surely hopes not only that some or another guest in the stone house will discover the source of his or her creativity, so to call it, but that she herself, impelled by the feeling of quiet intensity within the stone walls in the remote countryside, might discover what has been hitherto beyond her.

The interview with the author was broadcast several weeks ago. I have been able since then to observe several developments in my own thinking. Before I report these, I should point out that I have never learned to use any sort of electronic device. I am aware that the owner of a computer could have learned soon after the end of the radio broadcast the contents of the entire interview. Not owning a computer, I have to rely on my memory alone. While I was listening, the woman made no mention of the number of rooms in the stone house, and yet I saw in my mind just now a place where six or eight or even ten persons might have been comfortably accommodated. Admittedly, I have still not crossed the border, but I cannot believe that even a large farmhouse in the neighbouring state would contain more than four or five bedrooms. How then can I think, as I constantly do, of the woman's retreat as housing as many as ten writers or self-scrutineers?

I practised just now the sort of introspection that I suppose will be required of the residents of the stone house. I learned that my mental image of the house has expanded since I last inspected it or, rather, has accumulated around itself a set of satellite-images. Now, when I think of the house, I see at intervals around it where I formerly saw only lawns and flower-beds and an orchard, cabins or cottages of the same yellowish stone that the house consists of. The cabins are too small to have return verandas, but even without looking closely at the windows I know that at least one window in every cabin contains one or more coloured panes. The cabins are arranged as I supposed the cells were arranged in a certain community of monks that I read about perhaps forty years ago. The monks belonged to the Carthusian order, and their monastery was in a southern county of the country where fifteen of my sixteen great-great-grandparents were born, the same country in which was born the female proprietor of the stone house around the image of which are the stone cabins that are the subject of the previous sentence. The monks considered themselves a community but they met together on only one afternoon each week for a period of communal recreation: a few hours of strolling together or playing quoits or bowls. At all other times, each monk lived in solitude, praying or reading or writing or cultivating the vegetable garden that provided most of his food. The stone house, as it appears in my mind, has only four or five main rooms—far too few for the numbers of writers that I envisage as taking up residence there. The spacious rooms in the house, many of them with leadlight panes in their windows, are used for dining, for meetings, or for social gatherings. One such room is surely used as a library. Each inmate of the house studies, reads, writes, and sleeps alone in one or another of the outlying cabins.

The woman had no need to mention during her interview what all of her listeners surely understood: that the persons spending time in the stone house would be both men and women free, of course, from any restrictions arising from gender. I too understood this while I listened. In the presence of others, even if they be conjectured persons whose voices reach me only by way of my radio or my telephone, I think and feel in mostly conventional ways. Alone at my desk, however, and especially while writing a report such as this, I become what many would describe as an eccentric or a misfit. I had hardly begun to speculate about the stone house before I found myself devising the strict rules intended to keep mostly apart the men and women who would lodge there. Of course, mere rules could not prevent a man and a woman from meeting in private in his or her cabin if they so wished. In my version of things, however, any person who was attracted to the stone house and who was urged to investigate there the origins of his or her private imagery—any such person would be relieved to be free for the time being from close contact with another.

Still other details of the stone house owed nothing to what I had heard from the radio. The woman, as I now recall, had spoken of meetings and deep discussions. She would probably have had in mind a group of men and women seated informally around a table. I saw, from the first, a large room in which the light had been altered by its having passed through windows out of view of my mind's eye. The room was furnished with nothing resembling a table or chairs. The end of the room further from me was occupied by an organ loft. At the left and the right of my mental vantage-point were several rows of choir stalls, things that I had seen only in illustrations. The room was obviously a disused chapel of some kind, although I, its seeming architect or designer, was unable to see behind me the fourth of its sides, where was surely a bare altar.

Into the stalls mentioned step decorously the residents for the time being of the stone house, females to one side and males to the other. What happens next I am so far unable to visualise. Perhaps when the founder of the stone house has replied to my letter I will be better able to realise, in the original sense of that word, some of the impassioned yet decorous debates that might take place in that quaint but formal setting. Until then, the two groupings face one another silently and uneasily.

I mentioned a letter just now. For several days after I had heard the broadcast interview, I worked at composing a long letter to the author, the subject of the interview. When the letter was ready for sending, I called at the newsagency in this township, intending to have a copy made of the letter, but I was told by the newsagent that his copier, or the computer attached to it, was out of order. Perhaps rashly, I posted the letter there and then, after having addressed it in care of the radio station concerned. I reminded myself that I had on my desk several drafts of the letter. Those drafts are beside me now but they differ greatly. Even the latest few of the many scribbled pages seem far from explaining what I had set out to explain, and I hope that I omitted from my final draft certain passages that I cannot read nowadays without cringing.

In the meanwhile, no answer has reached me. If I assume that my letter was actually delivered to the addressee, then I am able to propose four possible explanations for my lacking a reply. The woman is perhaps like some of my former friends who transact all their business by electronic means and disdain to answer letters through the post. She may be one of those persons who claim always to be frantically busy and whose desk is always in disorder. In gloomy moments, I suppose that the woman has already decided not to reply to my letter because she found it vague or confused or even unseemly: she may even suspect its sender to be a tiresome eccentric or mentally unbalanced. In hopeful moments, I suppose her to be still composing one after another draft of her reply to a letter that she found thought-provoking and even engaging.

While I continue to wait for a reply, I sometimes resolve to consult my racing calendar and to choose a day when I might set out for some or another race-meeting in the adjoining state and might pass through district after district, seeing from the sides of my eyes one after another house likely to have attracted by now the notice of a person who spent her childhood on the edge of grasslands and who wonders about the sources of a certain sort of writing.

Sometimes I decide to wait for much longer before setting out across the border; to wait until the woman might well have bought and fitted out her chosen house and I am therefore free to think of her as waiting for insight on the far side of one after another wall of amber-coloured stone behind one after another return veranda of one after another house that I see from the sides of my eyes in one after another border district.

Sometimes I decide on what would be a bold move indeed from a person of my sort: I decide to turn these pages of handwriting into a neat typescript and to send the whole of this report, as I call it, to the woman mentioned often in its later pages—not in care of any radio station but to the postal address that I believe to be hers, which address I found recently in the telephone directory for the capital city of the adjoining state. I would send only a brief cover-note, carefully worded so as to suggest that the typescript is a work of fiction. And in case I should receive no reply even to that missive, I would have previously taken a copy of the whole so that I could have it by me whenever I travelled afterwards to one or another race-meeting in the adjoining state, watching from the sides of my eyes for a certain house; and so that I could turn in from the road if I saw the house and could stop my car on the sweeping driveway and could walk up the steps of amber-coloured stone onto the return veranda and could then stand in front of the door with a pane of coloured glass at either side, waiting to deliver my pretend-fiction to the person often mentioned in its later pages.

If ever I were to take the bold step mentioned above, I would first have to add several passages to the text as it now stands. While I was writing the previous pages, I sometimes left off writing about some or another matter in order to begin writing about some or another separate matter that had appeared just then at the side of my mind and might have disappeared if I had not begun at once to write about it, or so I thought at the time.

In connection with the single-volume history of English literature mentioned earlier, I would go on to report that I made no effort to read the book but looked often through it for the biographical details of a certain writer: not some or another writer known to me already but a male writer whose name I had not even discovered. As a young man, I was often driven to search thus not only for writers but for painters, sculptors, and composers of music who lived in isolation from their kind, far from the putative centres of culture. Even in my youth, I seem to have been seeking evidence that the mind is a place best viewed from borderlands. My school-prize yielded me three names of interest: John Clare, Richard Jefferies, and George Gissing.

In connection with the phrase *ice-green* that appears earlier in the report, I would go on to write about a certain evening when I was a small child and staying with my family as guests of three unmarried aunts and an unmarried uncle of mine in a house of pale-grey sandstone mentioned in the report. During that evening, the youngest of my aunts took me into the garden on the southern side of the house in order to have me view what she called the southern lights, which I remember as a roughly rectangular zone of green in the dark sky above the distant ocean and which my aunt explained as having been caused by the refraction of light from the midnight sun through numerous icebergs. My aunt and I might have watched the lights, so to call them, from the side of the return veranda if that place had not been blocked off by canvas blinds to form a sleeping-place for my uncle. Instead, she lifted me onto one of the blocks of pale-grey sandstone that formed a base beneath a tall rainwater tank. Later during my childhood, the tankstand, as it was called, became my preferred place for reading. The tank itself sheltered me from the wind off the ocean, and I was able while I read to touch the petals of the nasturtium plants that grew in crevices between the crumbling blocks of stone and were mostly of a colour between orange and red.

In connection with the phrase *ice-maiden* that appears earlier in the report, I would go on to write about the earliest instance that I can recall of my embracing a female person. The event took place during the last month of my twenty-first year. The weather at the time was hot, and the female person was lightly dressed, and what I recall most clearly is my shock at discovering that her bare flesh was warm to the touch whereas I had for long supposed that the flesh of female persons would have the feel of marble.

In connection with my one-time colleague, the author of a piece of short fiction about a priest obliged to mingle his urine with altar-wine, I would go on to write the following. After we had ceased to be colleagues, he and I rarely met. I did not even learn that he had died until a year after the event, when I received a circular letter inviting me to buy a copy of a book that had recently been published by a group of his friends and admirers. According to the circular letter, the author had been working on the book at the time of his death, and his widow had later finished the book as he had wanted to. I read also from the circular letter that the book was an utterly frank and candid account of the spiritual crisis that had caused the author to leave the priesthood.

I found the book tedious and self-serving, if not dishonest. I formed the impression that the author had finished writing the work long before his death but had not wanted to have it published in his lifetime lest certain passages should cause embarrassment to some of his elderly relatives, if not the author himself. These passages were an account of the author's having begun to masturbate for the first time after he had been an ordained priest for some years and while he was experiencing what the writer of the circular letter had described as a spiritual crisis. I had hoped that the book might reveal something of what I might have called the inner life of the author. I was curious to know what had taken place in the author's mind when he prayed or when he celebrated mass and later when he began to question whether he was called to be a priest and even, perhaps, to doubt the tenets of his faith. The book told me nothing about these matters. The author seemed unable to report anything but dreary debates between himself and his superiors, the architecture of the various religious houses where he worked as a priest, and the petty circumstances of his finally taking off his Roman collar and trying to dress and behave as a layman. I found it strange that a priest could write about his having masturbated but not about his having been in love with some or another image of his god.

In connection with the place-name that I have never been able to find in any gazetteer of the British Isles, perhaps I would go on to report something of what I learned during my most recent visit to the house mentioned often in these pages: the house where my bed stands beneath a bow-window bordered by coloured panes. The man who owns the house owns also a computer. During my most recent visit, and without my asking him to do so, the man typed into his computer, to use his own words, the place-name mentioned and then invited me to read a number of seeming pages that had appeared just then on the screen of the computer. The man offered to print out, as he put it, the seeming pages so that I could take them away with me afterwards, but I chose merely to read them on the screen, confident that I would later recall whatever deserved to be recalled. I learned from my reading that the place-name mentioned is a much earlier version of the present-day name of a small town in a border district of Scotland. I learned further that the small town was supposed to have been the birthplace, some centuries ago, of a man known as Thomas the Rhymer, who was supposed to have once visited Elfland in the company of the queen of that country or region and after his return to have sought continually to find his way back. I learned further still that the place denoted by the signpost that I have often passed was formerly one of the largest grazing properties in this state and that the double-storey homestead, which still stands, has in one of its walls a stone from the ruins of a tower that once stood in the place that bore long ago the name of the homestead and the surrounding property. I learned yet further that a more recent owner of the property with the double-storey homestead owned many racehorses, one of which, in the decade before my birth, won a famous steeplechase in the capital city where I was born.

If I were to report the items mentioned in the previous paragraph, then I would almost certainly go on to report the images that appeared to me while I was writing that paragraph, which images appeared as details in one after another pane of coloured glass in one after another window of a huge homestead on a vast grazing property, which panes were illustrations of dealings supposed to have taken place long ago between a man and a female personage in a district near a border.

In connection with the chapel that was the place of worship of the religious brothers who taught me at secondary school and was also the place where I sometimes paid a visit to a personage that I knew mostly as the Blessed Sacrament, I would go on to write that I looked several times into one or another of the bulky missals and prayer-books that rested all day on the seats of the chapel. Each of the brothers would have kneeled in his appointed place in the chapel during morning mass and whenever he and his fellows assembled during the day for prayers and would have left his books near by. Sometimes, if I was the only person in the chapel, I picked up the nearest book and looked at some of the many so-called holy cards poking out from between the pages of the book. (Sixty years ago, and for some years afterwards, priests and religious and pious lay persons amassed collections of such cards, being presented with them on birthdays, notable feast days, and anniversaries of ordinations, weddings, and such other events. A holy card had an illustration on its obverse side and a prayer or a pious invocation on its reverse.) I was curious to learn which so-called special devotions my teachers might have cultivated: what images they might have kept in mind while they prayed. I had little respect for the brothers who taught me. I considered most of them ignorant and incompetent teachers. And yet I was sometimes sorry for them on account of the drab lives they seemed to lead, and I would have liked to learn from my looking through their prayer-books that many a one of them was able to call up a rich and varied mental landscape whenever he prayed.

I remember only one of the cards that I looked at furtively. It belonged to one of the youngest of the brothers. I knew the man by name but he had never taught me. On the obverse of the card was a picture of the Virgin Mary. The pictured face was that of a young woman, hardly more than a girl, seemingly of Anglo-Celtic extraction and rather more fetching than the many similar illustrations that I had previously seen on holy cards. The reverse had been originally blank, but the owner of the card had written on it in pencil several resolutions of the sort that a zealous young religious of that era must often have written on the reverse of a holy card after having uttered the resolution in his mind as though in the presence of the personage depicted on the card. I long ago forgot all but one of the resolutions. That memorable item reads as follows. *Guard eyes while in town.*

In the early decades of the twentieth century, religious orders of priests or brothers or nuns mostly trained their postulants, novices, and professed students at some distance from the capital cities. The superiors of the religious orders seemed to have thought of the countryside as the best surroundings for young persons who might have been tempted to lapse from their religious zeal if they had been constantly exposed to the so-called distractions of city life. Some orders erected buildings of their own design on the outskirts of provincial cities or towns. Smaller orders bought and converted for their own use mansions built long before by wealthy pastoralists. The order of brothers under mention had as their training-house several newer buildings arranged around a mansion formerly owned by a leading family, so to call them, in a western district of the state adjoining the northern boundary of this state. Pupils of the brothers were sometimes shown photographs of their training-house. I can hardly recall the newer buildings that served as classrooms and dormitories, but I can see in mind still the building that comprised the brothers' residence and also the chapel: the two-storey building of stone surrounded on at least three sides by verandas on two levels. The verandas were bare in the photographs that I saw sixty years ago, but I see them now as shaded by many a vine-covered trellis and furnished in places with chairs and couches of cane. At one such place, a group of female persons is gathered as though to pose for a photograph. Some of the persons are elderly; others are hardly more than girls. Most are in white or pale-coloured dresses of a length long since unfashionable. A few wear wide-brimmed straw hats; others shade their eyes with their hands while they look towards the glaring paddocks in the mostly level grassy countryside.

For many years after I had first read the resolution on the back of the holy card mentioned above, I supposed that the author of the resolution had written it in comparatively recent times. I supposed that the town mentioned was his local suburb, through which he travelled each week to be umpire at school football or cricket matches. Or, I supposed that the town mentioned was the central part of the capital city through which he travelled by tram on certain afternoons when he had to attend as a part-time student some or another lecture or tutorial at the university. I supposed the man had wanted to guard his eyes against the sight of image after image of young women with bare legs and low necklines outside the cinemas that he passed. While I was writing the previous two paragraphs, however, I saw the writer of the resolution as writing it while he was still a young man, hardly more than a boy. I saw him as being still a student in the training-house of his religious order in a western district of the state to the north of the state where he later taught in an inner eastern suburb of the capital city. I saw him as writing on his card while he sat or knelt in the chapel of the building that had been formerly a mansion where lived one after another generation of pastoralists. The student, so I supposed, had wanted to guard his eyes on the two or three occasions each year when he travelled with his fellow-students on some or another holiday-excursion through the streets of some or another quiet township in the west of his state. He had not wanted to catch sight of some or another female face of the sort that he might have been likely to fall in love with. He wanted to remain true to the image lying between the pages of the book in his hands. When I first saw him writing, I saw above him a window of coloured glass installed by the order of brothers soon after they had occupied the building. One of the images in the window was of the same female personage whose image appeared on the obverse of the card that he was writing on. Soon afterwards, I saw above him one of the windows that the previous owners of the building had installed long before. The images in that window seemed meant to suggest stems and leaves and petals.

After I had finished my secondary schooling more than

fifty years ago, I made no effort to keep in contact with my former teachers or with any of my former schoolmates. Even so, I began to receive, a few years ago, copies of a periodical published by a society the members of which include some of my old schoolfellows. Someone, apparently, had supplied my address to the society. My habit is to leaf through the periodical looking for familiar faces among the reproductions of photographs of so-called old collegians at so-called functions and looking also among the lists of deceased old collegians for names of former classmates of mine.

The illustrations in the periodical mentioned show not only former pupils of my school but former teachers. I had heard from time to time during the decades when it was fashionable for priests and religious to break their vows—I had heard sometimes that this or that former teacher of mine had become a teacher in the state system or a truck driver or a volunteer in some or another African country. I would not have been surprised to learn that the order of brothers who had taught me had dwindled to a handful of aged men. Perhaps they have thus dwindled, but the few depicted in the periodical seem cheerful enough. I supposed also that the brothers would have long since discarded their black and white habit. So they have, but they still garb themselves distinctively in a cassock of white. I saw all in white in a recent issue of the periodical an image of the elderly man whose prayer-book I pried into long ago, he who had sworn to guard his eyes while in town.

In a recent issue of the periodical mentioned was an illustration showing an image of some or another window of stained glass in, I think, France. I have forgotten what I read in the caption beneath the illustration, but I recall clearly the subject-matter of the illustration. Depicted in the stained glass was the founder of the order of religious brothers mentioned often hereabouts together with the young men who were his first followers. Each young man is shown as wearing a robe of black with a white bib at his throat. None of these details surprised me, but I cannot account for each young man's being shown as having his eyeballs lying to one side: as looking from the sides of his eyes.

While I was writing the previous paragraph, I regretted that I have never been able to recall the details of the windows of the chapel in the grounds of my secondary school. I have no doubt that the windows were of coloured glass, but I recall only a certain golden or reddish glow inside the chapel.

While I was writing the previous paragraph, I heard in my mind two lines of poetry that I first read while I was a student at secondary school and have never since read. In one or another year of my secondary education, I was required to study three so-called Romantic poets. One was John Keats, some of whose poems I still recall. The other two were Gordon, Lord Byron and Percy Bysshe Shelley. I took a strong dislike to each of these two, partly as a result of my having learned something of their life-stories and partly on account of their poetry, which seemed to me fatuous and affected. And yet I foresaw, soon after I had begun to write this report, that I would be compelled to include in it a certain two lines from some or another poem by Shelley: lines that I had once found merely decorative and without meaning but have remembered for more than fifty years in spite of myself.

Life, like a dome of many-coloured glass,
Stains the white radiance of Eternity.

A Note About the Author

Gerald Murnane was born in Melbourne in 1939. One of Australia's most highly regarded authors, he has published eleven volumes of fiction to date, including *The Plains*, *Inland*, *Barley Patch*, and *Stream System*, as well as a collection of essays, *Invisible Yet Enduring Lilacs*, and a memoir, *Something for the Pain*. He is a recipient of the Patrick White Literary Award, the Melbourne Prize for Literature, and an Emeritus Fellowship from the Literature Board of the Australia Council. He lives in a small town in Western Victoria, near the border with South Australia.